To: MY special Friend
Torrie
Never [stop?] of
your Dreams and
always Believe in
Yourself

Alex P. Ueves

THE ADVENTURES OF PRINCE GABRIEL

by

Alex P. Veres

Bloomington, IN Milton Keynes, UK

authorHOUSE®

AuthorHouse™
1663 Liberty Drive, Suite 200
Bloomington, IN 47403
www.authorhouse.com
Phone: 1-800-839-8640

AuthorHouse™ UK Ltd.
500 Avebury Boulevard
Central Milton Keynes, MK9 2BE
www.authorhouse.co.uk
Phone: 08001974150

First published by AuthorHouse 2/2/2007

ISBN: 978-1-4259-8120-4 (sc)

Printed in the United States of America
Bloomington, Indiana

This book is printed on acid-free paper.

Cast of Characters

Prince Gabriel: Son of the King and Queen of Overon
King Thaylog: King of Overon
Queen Elbenor: Queen of Overon
Donella: Gabriels secret love
Sellion: the kingdom's Blacksmith and Donella's father
Avery: Gabriel and Donella's child
Mokochu: The spawn of Throntoc
Mako: a Dragoon Warrior from Inferno Valley
Vincent: an Archer from Greensdale
Kagan: a Dwarf warrior from the Sunset Hills
Throntoc: the Dark Lord of Overon and creator of Mokochu
Tiny: Mokuchu's pet Slytherin
King Portos: King of Inferno Valley
Queen Miria: Queen of Inferno Valley
Ackbar: King Porthos' evil Brother
The Great Dragon: Guardian of the Dragoons
Shegra: Mako's cousin
Catrina: Vincent's older sister
Capt. Andromados: the captain of the royal guards
The Copperheads: a band of bandits who rob the village
Blade: the leader of the Copperheads
Boirin: Kagan's brother
Scar: the Eagle Lord and Gabriel's old friend
Soraz: A powerful Necromancer from the Valley of the Dead
The Wraith Master: Soraz's most powerful warrior
Kendra: Princess of the Sprite kingdom of Sunniva
Whitney: Kendra's best friend
List: one of the royal knights and Kendra's secret love interest
Sar: an Ogre who collects Sprites, Fairies and Pixies
Clortho: Beast-Master of the kingdom of Seber and a highly skilled Mage

Hilda: Clortho's lovely assistant
Malcolm: one of Clortho's fellow performers
Prince Cedric: a noble Prince of the kingdom of Stilwell
King Valarian: Cedric's father and the King of Stilwell
Queen Edith: Cedric's mother and the Queen of Stilwell
Amelia: Cedric's beloved wife
Paige: Cedric's loyal squire
Brogan: an evil Mage who desires to take back the Ring of Souls

Settings and Locations

Overon: a magical kingdom ruled by King Thaylog Queen Elbenor and Prince Gabriel

Mount Gray Skull: Mokochu's hideout

The Marshlands: Home of Throntoc and Mokochu

Inferno Valley: Home of Mako and the Dragoons

The Sunset Hills: Home of Kagan and the Dwarfs

Greensdale: Home of Vincent

The Dewy Meadows: home of the Goblins

Snake Skull Mountain: home of Blade and the bandits

Treacherous Valley: the place where the Violet Stem grows

The Forest of Mists: resting-place of slain Dwarf warriors

The Valley of the Dead: home of Soraz

The Forbidden Tower: Soraz's headquarters

Greenwood Pass: location of the kingdom of Sunniva

Sunniva: Kendra's kingdom

The Swamp of Shadows: home of the Ogre Sar

Seber: home of Clortho

Stilwell: home of Prince Cedric

Contents

CHAPTER ONE

Rise of the Elf Prince

Many moons ago there was a magical kingdom called Overon where wondrous and mysterious creatures roamed the land; it was the most beautiful place in the whole universe. There were tall Willow-Trees that reached to the stars, there were beautiful flowers that came in all sorts of shapes, colors and sizes and there were all kinds of different folk that lived there.

There were tiny but beautiful Sprites, stout but strong Dwarf soldiers, cunning and mysterious Dragoon warriors and many others, all the people looked toward the kindhearted and watchful guidance of the royal family of Overon; King Thaylog and Queen Elbenor and for many years the people lived happily together. Then one day a terrible threat appeared in the kingdom of Overon, an evil demon named Throntoc arrived into the kingdom and unleashed his horrible fury upon the land.

At first the people tried to defend themselves but their efforts were futile and all hope seemed lost, but the King refused to give up. "I will not stand for this, I shall put a stop to Lord Throntoc's evil once and for all" King Thaylog stated, he then grabbed his sword and commanded his warriors to help him don his armor.

Once his armor was placed upon him the King raced out of the castle and hurried to the outskirts of his kingdom, where he saw Throntoc waiting for him; when Throntoc saw the weapon the King was holding he started to laugh mockingly at the sight of him. "HA-HA-HA-HA, do you really think that you can slay me with such a pitiful weapon?" Throntoc laughed, angered by Throntoc's insults the King charged toward him while grasping his sword tightly in his hands and swung it hard across Throntoc's chest.

When the blow connected with Throntoc's body the demon let out an ear-shattering screech, the blow left him both injured and confused. "H-h-how can t-t-this be, how could you hinder me when all other weapons were useless?" Throntoc asked in confusion. As the King stood back on his feet the light of the sun hit the blade and reveled that it wasn't an ordinary sword; unlike human swords the blade of King Thaylog's sword was made of a special type of crystal that existed in the caves of Mt. Talora.

"Now foul beast, leave here and never return" the King commanded, afterward he and the rest of the villagers returned to their homes, however unbeknownst to the King and his people Throntoc's evil was just beginning. "I-I-if you think that you are f-f-f-finished with me King Thaylog, you are sadly m-m-m-mistaken my dear friend" Throntoc said weakly, suddenly there was a loud blast from the sky and with the last amount of energy he had Throntoc created a more evil being to continue his plans.

"Now go my servant and continue my plans for total d-d-domination of the world and this t-t-time our people will prevail" he stated, "now I will g-g-give you a name, from this d-d-day fourth you shall be known as Mokochu." Mokochu then bowed to his fallen master and said, "I am at your command master, I will not fail you."

"Go now and lay waste to the world" Throntoc coughed, suddenly Throntoc's body transformed a pile of dust and a gust of wind began to blow his remains across the skies. Mokochu turned around and saw the kingdom of Overon below him; "enjoy your time of merriment while you can fools, I will return" Mokochu proclaimed, he then flew off to Mt. Gray Skull to begin his plans of attack.

<u>Years Later</u>

As the years passed the royal family was soon blessed with a beautiful young boy and the King and Queen named him Gabriel, he was a handsome young man with short, Raven-Black hair, Green eyes, he wore beautiful royal robes and though he was young he had a wonderful physique. He had a wonderful life in Overon, the servants treated him kindly, the townspeople loved and respected him and he had many friends in the village but he dreamed of leaving one day to explore the wonders of the world.

But the battle with Throntoc made not only the townspeople skeptic but the royal family as well, because of this Gabriel's parents promised themselves to never have their son put himself in any danger whatsoever. Sometimes Gabriel would ask if he would be allowed to join the Knights on special missions but the King and Queen would always refuse, even though Gabriel was sixteen years of age and was able to wield a weapon his parents were still very protective of him.

"I know that my parents mean well, I just wish they wouldn't keep me locked inside the kingdom so much" Gabriel thought, one day Gabriel was playing with one of his toy swords in his bed chambers and decided to stop and take a little break. He pecked his head outside his window and marveled at the view he had from his room when suddenly he saw a very familiar sight; it was the Blacksmiths' daughter Donella, she was the most beautiful She-Elf in all of Overon.

She had pale-white skin, long, black hair that measured below her shoulders and a finely crafted tiara around her head; she had a pair of beautiful violet colored eyes and wore a beautiful white gown. Gabriel had known her since they were children and as much as he dreamed of adventure he also dreamed of the two of them being together forever.

Suddenly there was a loud crash coming from the kingdom's entrance and the guards soon found out the cause, it was Mokochu and a band of Reptiliac warriors. "Good morrow to you, kingdom of Overon. Prepare yourselves for your annihilation" he laughed.

All the villagers were in a panic as the demons started to attack everything in sight, "that's right my brethren, leave no house untouched and crush all who stand in your way" Mokochu commanded. He then got up from his seat and floated high in the air toward the villagers, once Mokochu landed one of the local merchants dropped to his knees and begged Mokochu to spare them "please leave us be, we'll give you anything you wish. Gold, jewelry, silks. Anything" the merchant cried.

Mokochu looked at the man and laughed "BAH, I have no need for such useless material things. I have come to find a woman worthy enough to be my bride" Mokochu proclaimed. The entire village (especially the women) became disgusted by Mokochu's request; he then began to look over every woman in the village, after Mokochu reviewed every one of the females he lowered his head in disgust and prepared to announce his disapproval.

Suddenly Mokochu looked out in the crowd and saw Queen Elbenor standing next to the King, he then flew over to her and gave lustful chuckle. "Maybe if I add a few things like a little bit of scales, a horn and claws you might be the perfect woman for me" Mokochu said with a smile, when Mokochu began trailing his hand across her cheek the Queen bit his finger before he could continue any further. "OW, how dare bite my hand you miserable..." Mokochu suddenly stopped when he saw Donella hiding in her fathers shop, "my dear, you're the

4

most beautiful female I have ever seen. You shall make a much more appealing bride than that shaggy old witch" he stated while walking toward her.

Soon after hearing Mokochu's comment the Queen's anger started to rise, "SHAGGY OLD WITCH? WHY YOU GOOD FOR NOTHING WRETCH" she shouted but before she could do anything to him Mokochu grabbed Donella and descended back to Mt. Gray Skull. Gabriel could not believe what he'd just witnessed "N-O-O-O-O-O-O-O-O-O-O-O-O" he shouted and Mokochu was soon out of sight, Gabriel then fell on his knees and started to cry uncontrollably.

The guards looked at the Prince with concerned eyes "are you well my liege, you seem upset" one of them asked, the Prince slowly got back on his feet "upset, I'm not upset. I AM *FURIOUS*" he screamed. Some of the guards were frightened by Prince's reaction except for one, "'tis nothing to be upset about your highness, no one was harmed" the guard stated reassuringly.

Gabriel glared fiercely at the guard and grabbed him by the vest, "if you say those words again we shall *then* see if no one is harmed" Gabriel shouted. Everyone was shocked to hear the Prince speak in such a manner, then he bowed before his parents and looked at them with sad eyes.

"Please Mother and Father, I beg of you. Please allow me to go and rescue the Blacksmiths' daughter?" he asked but his mother didn't agree. "Nay Gabriel, I will not allow you to die for such a meaningless cause" she stated but on the other hand the King gave him permission to not only rescue her but also gather a band of other warriors to help him.

Later that evening Gabriel gathered warriors from all of Overon's neighboring kingdoms, warriors such as Mako of the Dragoon warriors of Inferno Valley, an Archer named Vincent from a village of humans called Greensdale and a Dwarf warrior named Kagan from the Sunset Hills. "My friends, for years my people have suffered greatly at the hands of Throntoc and his amphibious armies but now we face an even greater challenge, a being named Mokochu. I humbly ask of your assistance in not only defeating Mokochu but also in rescuing a young woman he has kidnapped, will you help me?"

All of the warriors nodded their heads in agreement "we will help you your majesty but may I ask you something?" the Dwarf named Kagan asked, The Prince agreed and the Dwarf asked him why the woman Mokochu captured was so important to him. Gabriel lowered his head then spoke "it is because… I love her, I loved here ever since the day we first met" he stated, he then started to think back many years ago to when they first met.

"I was but a boy at that time, I was happily racing through the gardens trying to catch Dragonflies when I suddenly ran into something. After I got back on my feet I dusted myself off and just when I was about to apologize my eyes met with the eyes of a young girl, I tried to say something to her but I froze and strange things started to happen.

My hands were shaking, sweat was dripping down my head, my heart was beating rapidly and I felt my knees growing weak, after I regained my composure and I apologized for running into her. We later introduced ourselves and shared a friendly conversation while I was walking her home, as the hours passed I decided to make my move. I was about complement her when suddenly my parents started calling me and I left just after I brought her home. After that day we saw each other whenever we could and I've been happy ever since" Gabriel concluded.

The Prince suddenly felt tears swell up in his eyes and he fell to knees and cried, "but now my happiness is gone, that accursed demon has taken her away from me to who knows where and I don't know if she's still alive. Please you must help me" Gabriel begged. The Dragoon warrior placed his hand on the Princes' shoulder and told him that they will not only find her but rescue her as well, later that night Gabriel and his team gathered whatever supplies they could carry and hurried over to Mt. Gray Skull.

When they arrived at the entrance of the mountain Gabriel and his team prepared for battle, as they reached the top they heard Mokochu torturing Donella inside his fortress. "It's useless to resist me so you might as well agree to be mine my dearest" Mokochu snickered, this made Donella so scared she started to cry but she soon stopped when she saw Gabriel pass by below the window.

Mokochu felt confused when he saw the cheerful look in Donella's face, suddenly Mokochu heard footsteps out on the wall and he soon spotted the Prince and his friends climbing near the window. "Well it seems that we have some company my sweet, what say we give them a warm welcome ha-ha-ha" he laughed, he then snapped his fingers which summoned a pack of his soldiers to the room "what is thy wish, O great one?" one of them asked.

Mokochu pointed his finger outside and said "take care of those intruders for me won't you?" Mokochu requested, soon after he made his command the soldiers left the room. Gabriel and his team of warriors soon made it to the front gate but just before they could continue forward Mokochu's minions arrived at the scene, "I fail to see how you worthless rabble could pose such a problem to Lord Mokochu" the tallest one stated.

"You'll soon find out if you don't tell me where Donella is" Gabriel said and then took a small step, the Reptiliac warriors quickly charged toward the Prince and the battle began. Each warrior fought a handful of demons with their most powerful techniques and maneuvers, Mako got rid of ten by using his combat techniques while Kagan swung his mighty battle-ax and Vincent used his bow and arrow.

Soon after the rest of the demons retreated the warriors were victorious and they congratulated each other with handshakes, suddenly they heard the sound of hands clapping coming from behind them. "Bravo gentlemen, you have successfully managed to defeat my most powerful minions. The real question is, do you have the courage and skill to face ME?" Mokochu shouted.

"Do what you will, if you kill us many other warriors will come fight you" Vincent said bravely but Mokochu just laughed, "ha-ha-ha-ha, oh heavens no. *I'm* not going to kill you all, that's *Tiny's* job" Mokochu stated. The Prince and his friends suddenly started to laugh "you're a crazy one Mokochu, do really think that we would fear something named Tiny?" Kagan chortled.

Suddenly the ground underneath them started to shake and then a giant Slytherin came rising out of the mote, the entire group stood dumb while Mokochu laughed evilly. "My friends, I would like you all to meet Tiny" he stated before pushing them off the tower and into the mote, Tiny started licking his lips hungrily at the sight of the warriors "if anyone knows how to get out of here I'm open for suggestions" Kagan shouted.

Gabriel thought for a quick moment and then asked for someone to toss him in the air above the Slytherin, Mako volunteered and once Gabriel was sent flying the beast started to chase after him. Unfortunately Tiny was so busy trying to catch Gabriel that he ended up hitting the wall in the process, when Tiny was knocked unconscious his large body created a way up for them.

Upon seeing this Mokochu became very angry "very good my friends, you now have my FULL ATTENTION" he snapped; he then saw the Prince standing beside the Dwarf. "Well-well-well it seems you've brought his majesty along with you, very good because I have a little friend of mine who is very anxious to see him" he chuckled fiendishly.

Mokochu pointed toward a high tower to reveal Donella tied to a pole, "let her go you fiend or by heaven I will make you regret the day you ever captured her" the Prince demanded. Mokochu glared at the Prince and shouted "DO YOU REALLY EXPECT ME TO COWER IN FEAR AT YOUR PUNY THREATS?" he then blasted a fireball from his hand at the Prince but Gabriel dodged it in the knick of time.

The battle continued for hours with neither one giving in, Mokochu fired blast after blast at the Prince but Gabriel was able to dodge all of them without breaking a sweat. Suddenly Mokochu delivered a powerful blow to the Princes' head that knocked him over the edge of the tower, but Gabriel was able to grab on to the wall.

"Well-well-well, you're really starting to try my patience boy" Mokochu shouted but what he didn't know was that Gabriel had his grandfathers sword with him, "no Mokochu, it is *you* are trying *my* patience. It all ends here" he screamed while unsheathing his sword. "If this blade worked for my ancestors it will also help me destroy you" Gabriel stated, he got back up on his feet and readied his blade.

"No you fool if you destroy me this whole fortress will fall," he screamed while frantically waving his hands, "that's what I am hoping for" Gabriel said fiercely. Gabriel then raised his sword high in the air and struck Mokochu across the chest but after he delivered the strike Mokochu grabbed Gabriels cape, "if I fall I'm taking you with me boy" he shouted.

Suddenly the fortress began to crumble and while the other warriors rescued Donella and escaped the Prince and Mokochu fell with the ruble, after the fortress collapsed and everyone made it to safety they all went looking for Gabriel until finally someone shrieked. "OH MY STARS, everyone I-I-I found him" Kagan said in shock, they raced over to Kagan and what they saw filled them with shock and terror.

They soon found the Prince lying unconscious in the ruble and everyone began to cry especially Donella, "wake up Gabriel, please wake up. Please Gabriel don't leave me" Donella cried. Finally Donella fell to her knees and cried on Gabriel's chest; suddenly Donella started to feel Gabriel moving in her arms, to her surprise Gabriel regained full consciousness without even a scratch on him.

"I-I-I don't understand, how could anyone survive that fall?" questioned Mako, Gabriel undid his shirt to reveal a vest made of a magic Elvish silk that was even stronger than Dragon scales. Everyone was happy to see that the Prince was unharmed and they soon returned to the palace to tell the good news, as soon as they arrived the King and Queen welcomed their son with open arms.

Later that day a celebration was held at the palace in honor of the victory over Mokochu and the wedding of Gabriel and Donella. "My son, you've made us very proud today. So in honor of your deeds I hear by make you a royal Knight" the King stated, soon everyone started to cheer loudly for Gabriel his friends began to congratulate him by patting him on the back and hugging him.

"Now you shall remain here and use your strength and skill to protect our kingdom" King Thaylog proclaimed, upon hearing his Fathers statement Gabriel lowered his head in sadness. "Nay Father, I cannot stay here" Gabriel said sadly, The King and Queen looked at him in surprise and asked "but my son isn't this what you wanted?" the Queen asked, "yes Gabriel, what more could you possibly want?" Mako asked.

Gabriel took a deep breath and answered "I want the world" everyone looked at Gabriel with concerned expressions, "I mean, I want to see the world, I can't stay here in the palace there's so many things out there to discover" Gabriel explained. His mother didn't agree, "I won't let you do any such thing" the Queen shouted. Before she could continue her husband stopped her, "nay my queen, we cannot do this. He's not a baby anymore" the King stated.

Soon the Queen began to cry loudly "but he is still my baby and what of your wife, do you think Donella is going sit still and wait for your return?" Donella gave a chuckle and stepped forward, "I most certainly will not… I'm going with you" she announced. The Queen was shocked but she understood Gabriel's wishes and gave him permission to leave, later that afternoon Gabriel and his companions were ready to leave.

The King and Queen stepped forward and each gave their son a loving hug, "know this my son, no matter where you are in the world you and your friends will always have a home here in Overon." Gabriel saluted his parents and they began to depart "do you think they'll be okay Thaylog?" the Queen asked, "I'm sure they'll be fine and I believe the rest of the other kingdoms of the world will be in safe hands as long as they're around, I'm sure of it."

As they left the kingdom of Overon Gabriel took one last look at his home before heading out on his next adventure and as they left Gabriel's horse let out a loud whiney while the others laughed and cheered happily. Gabriel then turned to his beloved Donella and gave her a kiss on her soft lips, "I promise you my love, someday when I bring peace back to the land we shall spend the rest of our lives happily together till the end of our days."

CHAPTER TWO

Wildfire

Many months have passed since Gabriel's victory over Mokochu and during that time he and his friends have become quite famous among the peoples of the Earth, after leaving his beloved kingdom behind the young Elf-Prince and his friends have traveled the world and had many adventures. They have defeated monstrous beasts, fought very powerful armies and have outwitted the most cunning of Wizards and warriors but soon the young warriors were about to embark on the first of their greatest adventures.

It was a peaceful morning in the valley of Sunset Meadows and the warriors decided to stop for a rest, many things have happened to the team such as the birth of Gabriel's son Avery and things seemed so peaceful that nothing would be able to ruin it. All of the sudden Mako spotted a small bird flying toward them, once it came near him Mako noticed a letter tied to its leg. Once Mako removed the note he began to read it and notice that the handwriting belonged to his Cousin Shegra, the note appeared to be some sort of urgent message.

It read:

"I have terrible news to bring to whosoever reads this message, as you may or may not know my Father Ackbar has been exiled from the Lotus Village and sent to the Black Mountains for twenty-seven years. But I fear that now he has returned and is now seeking his revenge upon my Uncle Porthos by kidnapping my Aunt Miria, I beg for your assistance in rescuing her and putting a stop to my fathers senseless attacks on my cousins village. My people I will be forever indebted to you if you except"

Please help us
Sincerely, Princess Shegra of Lotus Village

Mako could not believe it, in all the time he spent with his friends he had completely forgotten about his family and his village. He had never felt so angry at himself before and the rest of his fellow companions began to take notice, after reading the message Mako explained to the others that his home was in danger and they all agreed to help him rescue his Mother.

"I can't thank you enough my friends and if all goes as planned I will see to it that my parents reward you all handsomely" Mako stated, with all that said the brave warriors began their journey toward Inferno Valley. After five hours of traveling they've made it to Inferno Valley and just as they entered the village someone had spotted them *"Mako is that you?"* Mako looked behind him and what he saw made his eyes grow wide.

Standing before him was his cousin Shegra still looking pretty as he remembered when he was young; she had long black hair that measured to her hips, dark blue eyes, she wore a red dress and her hair was tied into a pony-tail by a gold ribbon. They soon leapt into each other's arms and they both appeared to be very glad to see one another, Mako then introduced his friends to her and Shegra smiled happily at he cousin's new friends.

"I'm very pleased to see that my cousin has made such wonderful friends, are you here to help us?" she asked, Mako and his friends all answered yes and Shegra was overjoyed. She then took them to the palace to meet the King but instead of seeing him greet them happily he was sobbing uncontrollably on his throne, "why, why would he betray us and take my Queen away?" the King cried.

When the King looked up and saw his son with his niece he stopped crying, "Mako my son, it's good to see a friendly face but I am very sorry. I cannot give you a warm welcome because... I fear that our guardian The Great Dragon has betrayed us" he stated. Upon hearing this news the color from Mako' face turned as white as snow while the others failed to understand what the King was saying, "who the devil is the Great Dragon?" Kagan questioned the King.

King Porthos looked at the Dwarf and responded "I suppose a proper explanation is in order, since you are my sons friends" he stated, he then took a seat back in his throne and began to tell the story.

<u>45 years ago</u>

"It all started many years ago when I was but a young lad, I was hiking through the woods when I was suddenly attacked by a band of Trolls. I ran as fast as I could but the Trolls finally caught up with me, and just when I thought it was the end a loud roar echoed like thunder in the distance. Suddenly a large creature rose to the skies, it was a giant Dragon with scales that were as bright as gold, its wingspan was bigger than my entire village and his steps seemed to make the whole Earth tremble.

When it landed it not only put the band of Trolls in shock it also struck fear in my heart as well, it let out a loud roar which caused the Trolls to quake with fear till finally they retreated. I couldn't help but stare in wonder at my savior, as most of you may know we Dragoons have always been allies with the Dragons of the Earth but this Dragon was different somehow.

After I told my father about what happened the Dragon began to help many other people from my village for many years, we were so grateful we dedicated a statue to him and made him the sacred guardian of our village."

"But now, for some unknown reason it seems that our guardian has betrayed us, at least that's what I think. Please, you must help us save our Queen and bring back our guardian. Will you and your friends help us my son?" he asked. They all understood and agreed to help, King Porthos then commanded his servants to prepare a delicious feast for them with all of Inferno Valleys greatest dishes.

After the feast was finished the King allowed them to rest in his home, the next mourning they all prepared to leave when Gabriel asked where is Ackbar's hideout was? The King pointed to the west to the Black Mountains, "that is where you will find them all, best of luck to you my friends. I'm counting on your safe return home, good luck my son" he stated, then Mako bowed before him and said "I will not fail you father."

As soon as they said their good-byes they began their journey toward the mountains unaware that someone was watching them, "sire, there are intruders heading toward our castle" one guard stated after looking into a magical looking glass. The mysterious figure got up from his throne and said "they must be coming from Lotus Village, find them and have them follow you here" the guards gave a bow then they left.

Mako along with his friends followed a path toward the mountains then without warning they were suddenly ambushed a band of the ugliest Ogres they have ever laid eyes upon, they each fought their best while Gabriel tried to protect his wife because she was holding a baby. Suddenly when one of the Ogres tried to attack Donella Gabriel began to chant an ancient spell he learned from when he was a young Elfling, "*Hasiptos Anos Pesupos*" Gabriel chanted.

At that moment a pack of vines came up and grabbed the Ogre in midair saving his wife and son in the process, after the fight with the Ogres they've made it to the Black Mountains unaware that someone was watching them. "Well-well-well Miria it seems that I have underestimated your son, it's time I've got reacquainted with my nephew" the stranger chuckled, the warriors went in the palace and began to search for the Queen when suddenly the room completely lit up.

"Hello Mako, it's so nice to see you. I see you have some new friends with you, you'll need them in order to stop this" Ackbar stated, then he snapped his fingers and something began to rise out of the floor which made Mako's eyes grow wide, it was the Great Dragon roaring and stomping ferociously. "So *this* is your Great Dragon Mako, it doesn't seem very happy to see us" Kagan stated; Ackbar then laughed mockingly at the warriors' fear, "that is correct my friends, because I couldn't attack Mako's village on my own I realized that I needed some special help. Then I remembered all of the stories the people told about the Great Dragon so I went to see for myself if he was real."

Mako glared at his uncle and shouted, "so once you've located our guardian you used your sorcery to take control of his mind, you're even more evil than Father and Mother said you were" he said angrily. He suddenly remembered about his Mother and started to get even angrier but all his Uncle did was smile, "I know what you're thinking my dear nephew but I'm afraid your Mother can't see you right now because she's a little *tied up* right now" he laughed.

He then showed the group where the Queen was; she was locked inside a cage hanging over a pit of very hungry swamp creatures "you see Mako, you should be more concerned about rescuing your dear Mother instead of trying to defeat me" Ackbar said while laughing. This made Mako even angrier than before, suddenly Vincent reached over tapped Mako on his shoulder "Mako, we'll keep him occupied while you go rescue your Mother" he whispered but Mako looked at him confused.

Mako's confusion soon disappeared when Gabriel revealed a small smoke bomb hidden inside of his vest; Ackbar raised an eyebrow and tried to figure out what they were planning, suddenly he and the Great Dragon became blinded once Gabriel threw his smoke bomb. This gave Mako the perfect opportunity to rescue his Mother, he tossed one of trusty throwing stars at the rope that tied the cage, jumped underneath it and carried it to safety.

As soon as he regained his eyesight he saw the Queen out of the cage, "why you insignificant little whelps" he shouted then he commanded the Dragon to attack the warriors. The beast let out a loud roar as he stampeded toward them but then he stopped as Mako raised his hand, "don't do this to us, we're your friends. *He's* the real enemy" he stated while pointing at Ackbar.

The Dragon started to feel very strange, at that moment the Great Dragon grabbed his head and began to screech loudly. Apparently his own willpower was struggling against Ackbar's dark magic but before he could break free the Sorcerer gave him a stronger doze of his magic. "Do not listen to him, *he's* the enemy not me" he shouted but the Dragon soon regained control, once he returned to normal the Great Dragon glared angrily at him and gave a low growl.

"You impudent little dog, HOW DARE YOU TREAT ME LIKE SOME KIND OF PUPPET" the beast screamed, the Dragon let out a roar so loud the entire castle started shake, once the Dragon heard the rumbling he realized it was time to leave. "This entire castle is beginning to collapse, we must leave" the Dragon stated, the Dragon gathered all the warriors onto its back and flew out the window but suddenly Ackbar grabbed onto the Dragons tail.

"Oh no you don't" screamed the Queen as she started stomping on Ackbar's hand, he tried to keep a strong grip on the tail but he soon lost his grip and fell to the ground. A half an hour later the warriors along with the Great Dragon arrived back at the village, but the townspeople didn't seem too happy to see him.

"All is well my people, our guardian's mind was taken over by my Uncle Ackbar, but his hold over him is now broken" Mako proclaimed, the townsfolk looked deeply into the Dragons eyes and saw that his mind was cleansed of all evil thoughts. They were so happy for the return of their guardian that they all cheered while the Queen happily ran into her husbands' arms; the King released her and asked his son what happened to his brother.

Mako explained that when the Dragon returned to normal it became angry and caused the whole castle to fall, then when the Dragon began to fly out the castle Ackbar grabbed on to its tail and tried to escape with them but the Queen knocked him of the Dragon. The King was relieved that their guardian returned to normal and the whole village held a big celebration in their honor, later that night the warriors were ready to continue their journey but the King was concerned.

"Are you sure you and your friends don't want to stay here my son, with your skills you can do a lot of good here" the King asked, Mako placed his hand on his fathers shoulder and smiled. "Our village has you and our great warriors father, there are other places where we can be of more help" Mako stated, his father understood and said his good-byes to his son and his friends.

Suddenly as Gabriel and his friends began to depart Shegra quickly raced into the room, "if you and your friends are going on another adventure there's one thing you have to take along" she explained. "What's is that, dear cousin?" Mako asked, Shegra then raised her arms and said "me, I would love to come along with you. If it is alright" Shegra requested.

They all agreed and once their good-byes were said Mako and his friends left on their next adventure but everyone couldn't help but wonder about what happened to Ackbar, meanwhile back at the Black Mountains a dark figure came out of the rubble and laughed loudly. "If you think that you and your friends are through with me, you are sadly mistaken my young friend. Ha-ha-ha-ha-ha-ha-ha-ha-ha"

CHAPTER THREE

Race Against the Hourglass

It was a sunny and peaceful afternoon as Prince Gabriel and his friends took the opportunity sit back, relax and enjoy the quiet scenery; Mako spent his freetime practicing his Martial Arts, Kagan polished his axe and Gabriel spent some much needed quality time with his wife and child. Suddenly the serene atmosphere was disturbed when Vincent looked out into the distance and saw a cloud of dust heading toward them; he looked closer into the cloud and saw a pack of hooded horsemen riding passed them as if they were being chased by a horrible creature.

"What the devil, where did they come from?" Kagan asked in shock, they soon got back to walking on their way when Vincent saw a very familiar sight. "Look straight ahead everyone" Vincent shouted, Gabriel and the others looked in the direction Vincent was pointing and saw the Kingdom of Greensdale.

Vincent couldn't help but feel teary-eyed when he saw his home even though he was gone for a year but what he and his friends didn't know was their next adventure awaited them over the next rise. Once they've entered the village all the shops suddenly closed up and all the people started running around trying to find hiding places, Kagan suddenly spotted a small shop that was still open and raced over to it to buy supplies.

When the clerk saw them walking toward his shop he gave them all an angry glare, "away with you vile fiend, haven't you and your friends done enough damage?" the clerk shouted. The clerk then noticed the tall man standing behind the Dwarf and his eyes immediately grew wide, "Sir Vincent, is that you?" the clerk asked.

Vincent nodded his head and the clerk raced out of his shop, "everyone I have wonderful news, our beloved Sir Vincent has returned to us" he shouted. When Vincent and the others stepped out of the shop the whole village let out a loud cheer at the sight of their dearest friend, at that moment someone else came racing out of the crowd, "brother, is that you?" the woman asked.

Vincent looked ahead of the crowd and spotted his older sister Catrina racing into Vincent's arms, "my dear sister, 'tis grand to see you after so long" he said cheerfully. Vincent then faced his friends and introduced the woman to them, "everyone this is my older sister Catrina" he stated.

Catrina was a tall elegant woman with long golden hair, green eyes, a golden tiara and a beautiful green and gold dress, Gabriel and his friends all bowed their heads in greeting along with Catrina. After they said their greetings Vincent asked why the people in the village were behaving so strangely, she lowered her head in sadness and began to tell the story. "I'm sorry to tell you this my dear brother but our parents are very sick with a dreadful virus along with half of the village, then a band of hooded riders came and stole almost all of our Kingdom's medicine."

Vincent was shocked when he heard the news along with his friends, "who would do this to our village?" Vincent asked in shock. Catrina told him of a pack of bandits known as the Copperheads, "ever since they arrived in our village they have done nothing but torment our people for their own amusement" Catrina stated coldly.

She then explained that there was only one hope for Greensdale, the thieves stole most of the medical supplies but they left a few things behind for the people to make the antidote. There was one thing they needed to complete the antidote and that was to find a plant known as the Violet Stem flower, Catrina then pointed toward a place called Treacherous Valley.

"That is where you will find the Violet Stem but be warned, the bandits are very dangerous and their leader is even worse than they are" she stated, Vincent assured Catrina that he and his friends would be perfectly safe. After all explanations were said Catrina and a few people from the village gave her brother and his friends a wonderful meal as a token of thanks, suddenly another person appeared from the crowd to greet Vincent.

"*Ha, it's been a long time. Hasn't it Sir Vincent?*" a voice called out from behind, it was the Captain of the royal guards Capt. Andromados and Vincent's closest friend. "Is that really you Captain?" he asked in excitement, then both Vincent and the Captain gave each other a hug in greeting Vincent introduced his friends to the Captain.

"It's very nice to meet you all and I'm glad to hear that you're going to help my friend in finding the Violet Stem and save our village" the Captain said happily. Later the next day they set out toward Treacherous Valley and the Violet Stem, suddenly as they traveled through the woods a band of Trolls jumped out in front of them.

"Well-well mates, looks like we've got some friends to have for dinner" one Troll laughed, Kagan stepped forward and thanked the Trolls for the invitation but the Trolls suddenly started to laugh. "You must've misheard us lads, we're not having you *to* dinner, we're having you *for* dinner" another Troll stated, the demons licked their lips hungrily and charged toward the warriors; some of them were using torches to trap them while others waved their swords frantically in the air.

They all tried to think of a way out of this situation and then Gabriel came up with an idea, he raised his hands in the air and a strange light started to form in his hands. *"Aquarous Airous Maybron"* Gabriel chanted, at that moment water shot out of his fingertips and crashed into the Trolls.

Once the Trolls were defeated Gabriel and his friends continued on with their journey, "Blade is not going to like this at all mates, he's going to have our heads when we tell him" one of the Trolls said fearfully. Feeling both afraid and humiliated the Trolls returned to Snake Skull Peak to tell their leader the news, "I am *most* displeased, I had that village in the palm of my hands and now you tell me you've been defeated by a pack of low class warriors" their leader growled.

He stomped forward and grabbed one of the Trolls by the neck; "I will not tolerate failure any longer, so I will give you one more chance. Destroy these interlopers OR ELSE!" he shouted, "or else what o fearless leader" one of them said sarcastically. Once he set his minion down the Troll's leader took out a big slab of meat from behind him and threw it in the water surrounding his throne, when the meat landed in the water a pack of vicious piranha ate it in less in a second.

The Trolls were shocked when they saw the fish feasting so savagely, "or else *that*, so what's it going to be?" questioned the Troll's leader. As if on queue the Trolls raced out of the room and into the forest with quick pace, meanwhile Vincent and his friends were passing through the Dewy Meadows completely unaware of the Trolls watching them.

"Here they come mates, you know what to do now?" the lead Troll instructed, the other Trolls nodded and when the group passed by them they pounced. "Halt puny creatures, give up and we promise to eat you quickly" one of them shouted, even though they seemed fierce Gabriel noticed that they didn't seem that smart.

Gabriel clasped his hands together and created a small fire spark, the Trolls looked at them confused then Gabriel tossed the spark at their heads. "Watch out, it's a firefly" the stout-looking Troll screamed, at that moment the Trolls soon started swatting at each other which immediately led to them hitting each others faces.

"Ouch, that's my nose you just smacked you blinking imbecile" the tall one shouted "well *that* was me eye you dumbbell" the one with a pink eye screamed, while the Trolls were busy hitting each other the warriors continued toward Treacherous Valley. Unbeknownst to the warriors the Troll's leader sat upon his throne watching over them in anger through a looking glass, "I should have learned, never send Trolls to do an Orc's job" he stated.

The warriors soon made it through Treacherous Valley and soon came across a big door with a Gargoyle's head in the middle, they all tried as hard as they could to open the door but failed then suddenly they heard a voice. "*To pass though this door, complete this task, you must try to answer whichever riddle I ask. I always run but never walk, I have a mouth but I never talk*" the head stated, the others all thought as hard as they could to answer till finally Gabriel figured out the answer.

"I know what it is, the thing that runs but doesn't walk and has a mouth but doesn't talk is a river" he stated, the gargoyle's eyes stopped glowing and the door slowly started to open. "How did you know the answer Gabriel?" Donella asked, Gabriel told his wife that his father told him the same riddle when he was a boy.

Unfortunately he couldn't figure it out so quickly at such a young age but after his father told him the answer he knew it by heart, once the door opened they've entered a small garden where the Violet Stem flowers were supposed to be. To their surprise however the flowers were missing, " I believe that you are looking for *these* gentlemen" a voice laughed.

They all turned around to see an ugly green Orc standing behind them wearing brown pants, a black cloak and he was also holding a handful of the Violet Stem flowers in his left hand. The Orc soon noticed Vincent standing beside the Dwarf, "good day Vincent, how good to see you" the Orc laughed.

"It's good to see you again as well Blade, I see you're still missing that arm of yours" Vincent stated, his friends looked at him confused and asked Vincent how he and the Orc knew each other. "Who is this creature and how you know him?" Shegra asked, Blade looked at her with an evil look in his eyes "he fought me ten years ago my good woman and I haven't forgotten him ever since he cut off my arm and forced me to replace it with this accursed blade" Blade growled.

As he moved his cape off his right arm it revealed a long and bloody sword attached to his shoulder, "now that you're here Sir Vincent I can finally get my revenge" he stated. Suddenly Blade lashed out toward the warriors with his sword-like arm; "Donella, you must leave here and keep our child safe" shouted Gabriel.

Once Donella fled with her baby Gabriel began to fight, however despite the brave efforts of he and his friends Blade countered every attack and sent it back tenfold. Suddenly Mako took out a small bottle from his pocket, drank it and let loose a massive blast of fire from his mouth, all was quiet for a moment then a shadowy figure stepped out of the flames.

"HA-HA-HA-HA is that the best you've got? You've barely singed my leg hairs" a voice laughed, strangely enough that remark came from Blade. He then let out a large blast of energy so powerful it knocked everyone to the ground, "well my old friend, you've really disappointed me. I've really expected better of you during our time apart, any last words before I put you and your friends out of your misery?" Blade asked.

Vincent then looked above Blade and spotted Donella, "ha-ha-ha, yes I do have something to say. Watch your head" he chortled. Blade turned around only to have a large rock hit him square in the face, after he fell to the ground Vincent and the others grabbed the flowers and left.

However it seemed to be far from over, once Blade regained consciousness he was not happy about what happened. "If you think that this game is over, I fear that it's just beginning my young friends" Blade stated, he then pulled out a whistle from his pocket and blew on it. As Gabriel and the others continued their way out of the valley everyone soon heard movement from somewhere in the thicket, suddenly a pack of hungry Wolf-Dogs leaped out of the bushes and attacked Gabriel and his friends.

But for some reason Gabriel didn't seem worried; "I know how to deal with the likes of them" Gabriel laughed, the young Elf suddenly pulled out a small Pan-Flute and started to play a very melodious Elvish tune. The Dogs soon stopped running and soon started to fall asleep, once the Dogs were sound asleep Gabriel and his friends continued running.

Suddenly Blade appeared in front of them and growled ferociously, "if you believe you will leave here unscathed you are sadly mistaken" he said angrily. He raised his blade high in the air and swung it at the group but Mako pulled out a bottle, drank it and melted the blade with a blast of fiery breath, "why you little whelp, I'll make you pay for what you did to my arm" he shouted.

Suddenly Gabriel and Donella appeared and threw a net over him, once he was caught Vincent and his friends journeyed back Greensdale with the Violet Stem flowers and Blade in hand. When they all returned to the village they gave the flowers to the medicine men to make the antidote, after one hour of waiting the doctors came in to inform the warriors of the situation.

"Thank the stars you and your friends returned on time, otherwise all would have been lost. It's seems everyone is going to be fine, including your parents Vincent" one medicine man stated. They all let out a loud cheer of joy but Vincent stopped when he saw his parents ahead of him, "I'm so happy you are well Mother and Father, I thought I have lost you" he cried when he ran to hug them.

"All of Greensdale owes you and your friends a great debt of gratitude my son" Vincent's Father stated, later that evening a feast was held in honor of the deeds done by Vincent and his friends and after the feast was eaten the warriors decided it was time to leave. At that moment Capt. Andromados and Catrina came rushing over to them, "halt Vincent, you cannot leave without me and your sister. I insist that you take us with you, after all I *am* your commanding officer" he the captain chuckled.

Vincent nodded his head along with the others and they excepted the Captain as a part of their group, once that was settled they all set out on the next adventure. Meanwhile back in Greensdale, Blade was stomping around in his cell with anger swelling up inside of him.

"Once I get out that accursed huntsman will be mine, if I ever *do* get out of here" he stated, suddenly a hooded figure came up to his cell door and used some kind of strange power to break the lock. "Oh I believe that you'll fight him sooner than you think my friend" a strange voice laughed, once Blade was free the stranger and a bunch of other hooded figures left the jail and went on to find another warrior to help them.

"Once I get enough warriors to help me Gabriel and his miserable friends will perish. Soon Greensdale, Overon and every Kingdom in the world will be mine" the voice laughed.

CHAPTER FOUR

The Wrath of the Dead

After Gabriel and his friends said their good-byes to the people of Greensdale they gathered up their supplies and continued on their journey, they journeyed over mountains, sailed over the most treacherous of waters and fought against the most gruesome creatures they have ever seen. Five months went by and everyone soon started to grow weary, "if we don't find a village soon I will surely waste away to nothing" Mako cried.

"You have nothing to complain about Mako, you're not the one trying to protect a baby" Donella shouted, after that statement was said Mako and Donella soon broke out into another argument. Remembering Mako's unbelievable strength Gabriel tried to break the two up as quickly as possible, "Nay, stop your quarrelling this instant, this is no way for friends to behave" Gabriel stated.

"I know that all of you are tired and hungry but fighting isn't going to help with any of our problems, there might be a village up ahead if we just have to keep looking" Gabriel informed, suddenly the group heard the sound of a bird calling. "Kagan seems to have found something, make haste everyone" Vincent shouted, when they arrived at the hill where Kagan was they looked toward the horizon and saw a hideous site.

In front of them was a forest filled with decaying trees and a nearly destroyed gateway with dozens of Dwarves trying to rebuild it, "what is this place?" questioned Donella. "This is… my home" Kagan said in shock, the warriors looked at Kagan in both shock and confusion while Kagan fell to his knees and cried.

Suddenly a voice cried out from the distance *"Kagan, is that you little brother?"* the voice asked, when Kagan heard the voice he immediately raced through the main gate and began searching every corridor of the palace for the source. At first he had no luck in finding the mystery caller till finally a Dwarf came running toward the group, "you *are* alive Kagan, thank heavens" the Dwarf cried.

Kagan looked in amazement at the sight of his older brother alive and well, "Boirin my friend, it's grand to see you alive and well" Kagan stated happily. While Kagan continued to greet the Dwarf happily Gabriel and the others stared at them in confusion, "do you know this Dwarf Kagan?" Vincent asked.

Kagan gave a nod and introduced the Dwarf to the others, "everyone, this is my older brother Boirin. Boirin these are the friends I've met in my travels" Kagan stated. Gabriel and his friends all said their greetings and asked Kagan what happened to his village, "a powerful Necromancer named Soraz came and attacked our home without warning, at first we tried to defend ourselves but our attempts were useless" Boirin stated.

Kagan growled angrily and kicked a huge stone across the field, "I'm sorry to here about what happened to your home my friend, is their anything we can do?" Donella asked. "Of course there's something we can do lassie, tell us Brother where we might find Soraz and we'll destroy him" Kagan said angrily, Boirin nodded his head and pointed toward the East.

"Travel toward the East and you will come across a dark structure, it is known as the Forbidden Tower and that is where you'll find Soraz"

Boirin answered. After gathering the proper supplies Gabriel and his companions began their journey toward the Forbidden Tower, as the warriors continued their journey the soon started traveling through an area known as the Forest of Mists.

"Where the devil are we, I have a horrible feeling about this place" Catrina asked fearfully, Kagan laughed loudly and said "there's no reason to fear this place my lady, this is the Forest of Mists. This is where the most noble warriors in the Sunset Hills have fought, it is also considered to be the resting place of slain Dwarf warriors but there's no reason to fear."

Suddenly Gabriel's sharp Elf-ears picked up a soft rumbling sound in the distance, the rumbling then started to grow louder and louder till finally a pack of skeleton warriors wearing Dwarf armor appeared. "What was that you were saying about having no fear of this place Kagan?" Captain Andromados said smugly, after hearing the Captain's statement the skeletons turn toward him and attacked.

The skeleton warriors growled hideously as the continued to swing their weapons franticly, suddenly Donella tripped over one of the trees roots and fell backwards. Before Donella could move one inch one of the skeletons placed his sword on her neck and prepared to strike, at that moment Donella's son Avery began to cry loudly.

"My wife and son are in danger, I must to their aid" Gabriel shouted, he then pulled out his sword and raced as fast as his legs could go. "Back away from her you vile thing" Gabriel growled, upon hearing the young Prince's voice the skeleton took his attention off of Donella and faced Gabriel.

The demon glared at the Prince and started to laugh in a very raspy voice, the skeleton then lifted its axe high up into the air and swung numerous times with all its might but Gabriel somehow managed to dodge every strike. *"This has gone on for far to long, I must rejoin the others"* Gabriel thought, the young Elf-Prince clutched his sword tightly in his hand and delivered a power blow to the skeletons head. The blow successfully defeated the demon but the soon Gabriel and his friend were soon overpowered by more undead creatures, "this bodes ill my friends, it has been an honor to fight beside you" Kagan stated.

"Hold, it is *far* from over my friend. We are not alone in this fight" Gabriel said while pointing at the sky, suddenly Gabriel and his friends were quickly snatched up by a flock of huge Eagles and carried off into the skies. "Where the deuce did these Eagles come from and what do they want with us?" questioned Kagan, "do not fear everyone, these creatures are our friends" Gabriel said, after what seemed like endless hours of flying Gabriel and his friends finally landed at the edge of the Forest of Mists.

"It is wonderful to see you again Scar, many thanks to you for rescuing us" Gabriel said cheerfully, "there is no need for thanks young Prince, your family saved mine many years ago and I promised that I would someday repay them" Scar stated. With that statement made Scar and his flock began to fly back to the skies, "farewell Prince Gabriel, may your journey be a smooth one. Perhaps our path will cross again someday" Scar stated.

As Scar and his Eagle brethren began to disappear from sight Donella looked behind her and shrieked at the site before her, "what is the matter Donella?" questioned Gabriel. Donella slowly raised her hand and showed her friends the site that frightened her, before them was a bleak and desolate wasteland with dried up riverbeds, dead trees and scattered remains of thousands of warriors. In the middle of the wasteland stood a tall, dark tower covered with spikes and a mote filled with a foul-smelling liquid that made even the mightiest creatures quiver in disgust.

"What is this place?" questioned Mako, Kagan gave a low growl and answered by saying "This used to be a very beautiful place, but the evil of the Necromancer drained all the beauty from it. Now many of my people call this place the Valley of the Dead," the warriors looked around the valley and spotted the tower in the middle of it.

"That must be the Forbidden Tower, the Necromancer must be inside. Make haste everyone" Gabriel stated in disgust, as the warriors inched closer to the tower they soon started to smell the rancid odor from the mote. "I have never smelled anything so foul in my life, no creature alive could bear this stench" grumbled Vincent, Gabriel quickly tore off a piece of his cape and wrapped it around his face.

After carefully wrapping the cloth around his face Gabriel looked at his companions and instructed them to do the same, "we must press on my friends, do not let the stench hinder you" Gabriel stated. Once his companions were well protected from the stench the only thing Gabriel tried to think of a way into the tower, after what seem a few moments of thinking Gabriel came up with an idea.

"Vincent, Capt. Andromados, fire your arrows at the chains beside the drawbridge" Gabriel said while pointing at the bridge, the two Archers found the target that Gabriel spoke of and fired two arrows at the chains. When the arrows hit their target the drawbridge fell to the ground with a loud "THUD," once the bridge was lowered Gabriel and his friends began to cautiously enter the tower.

"This is too easy, where is the challenge in all this?" Kagan laughed loudly, suddenly the wall exploded and a gigantic warrior wearing black armor and a three-horned helmet stepped forward. "What the devil is this abomination?" Donella asked frightened, the warrior gave a low and raspy chuckle and said "I am the Wraith Master, Soraz's most powerful warrior and you shall not take one more step."

The young Prince and his companions prepared themselves for battle as the Wraith Master pulled out his sword; the Wraith Master's sword was six feet long and had jagged spikes on the sides, "I think we may be in over our heads here" Capt. Andromados stated. The Wraith Master lifted his sword high above his head and swung it full speed at the warriors, thinking quickly Gabriel and his companions dodged the attack but Donella accidentally dropped her child in the process.

When Avery landed on the ground he began to cry very loudly, when the Wraith Master heard the baby he decided to silence it forever. "You miserable little wretch, I'll see to it that your cries are silenced for good" the Wraith Master growled, when Donella finally regained her balance her eyes grew wide with horror at the site before her.

"Gabriel, Avery's in danger. You must save him" Donella shouted, Gabriel quickly turned behind him and raced toward his small child at full speed. As the Wraith Masters blade inched closer to the ground Gabriel slid on his stomach toward them and successfully snatched his child up in his arms, "I won't let you harm a hair on this child's head you monster" Gabriel growled.

"Vile Elf-Prince, you shall pay for interfering" the Wraith Master stated, the two warriors looked angrily into each other's eyes and prepared for battle. "I must warn you, this sword has been passed down throughout my family for generations, it has never failed us in battle" Gabriel said proudly, soon the whole room echoed with the Wraith Masters evil laughter.

"*Your* sword may have not failed you in battle but neither has *mine* my friend" the Wraith Master laughed as he charged forward, the battle waged on for two hours with neither warrior giving up. Finally both warriors gathered what little strength they had left to deliver one final blow, both the Wraith Master and Gabriel slowly stood back up on their feet and began to charge toward each other.

"Prepare to meet you doom, Knave" the Wraith Master roared, suddenly the two warriors leapt high into and slashed each other with their most powerful attack. When the attack was made Gabriel and the Wraith Master stood silent for what seemed like eternity till finally the Wraith Masters helmet slipped off his head and his whole body fell to the ground.

"Well played Gabriel, very well played" Vincent commented while patting Gabriel on the back, at that moment a black energy field took form around them and they were soon transported to another area of the tower. When the energy field was gone Gabriel and his friends soon found themselves in a very mysterious room, "where the devil are we?" questioned Kagan.

Before anyone could answer Kagan's question the room suddenly echoed with fiendish laughter, "so, you've defeated the Wraith Master? You must be very strong warriors to accomplish such a feat" the voice laughed. The warriors moved their heads around frantically while trying to find the source of the laughter, "who are you and what do you want with us" Gabriel shouted.

At that moment a dark vortex appeared in the middle of the room and an elderly man began to step out of it, "I am Soraz, the most powerful Necromancer in all the land and once I dispose of you I shall rule the world" Soraz proclaimed. The old man had a wrinkled face, a long white beard, long, wrinkly fingers with claw-like nails and wore a dark purple robe, Soraz then grabbed his black scepter and began to power up his magic.

"Try to escape *this*, fools" Soraz stated while firing numerous shots at them, though Gabriel was feeling weak from his battle with the Wraith Master he still managed to successfully dodge all of Soraz's attacks. "You cannot keep this up Elf, soon you will grow weaker and that's when I will have you in my clutches" Soraz chuckled, suddenly Gabriel tripped over one of the spell books that were on the floor and fell to the ground.

Gabriel tried to get back on his feet but his body was too weak to move even an inch, "prepare to join the others in the Spirit World" Soraz cackled. As Soraz prepared to deliver the final blast Kagan smashed his axe in Soraz's back; "I will not let you harm my friend as long as I have strength within me" Kagan growled, after the blow was delivered Kagan helped Gabriel back to his feet.

"Thank you for saving me my friend, bless you for having such strong arms" Gabriel said happily, "bless *you* for having such great courage and inner strength, any other being would have surrendered immediately" Kagan laughed. After Gabriel regained his balance he and his companions looked on in amazement as Soraz slowly began to disappear, as the Necromancer began to vanish he made one final statement.

"Do not think that this will be the last you'll see of me, I shall return one day and I will have my vengeance" Soraz stated as his voice echoed throughout the room, when the Necromancer disappeared all was silent for a moment. Suddenly Donella's Elf ears picked up a low rumbling sound from above them, "the whole tower's coming down, we must make haste for the gate" Donella shouted.

After hearing Donella's statement Gabriel and others quickly made their way toward the main gate of the tower, when they all successfully made it though the gate the tower fell to the ground in pieces. "We did it everyone, we defeated the Necromancer. My people are safe once again" Kagan stated, moments later Gabriel and the others all returned to Kagan's village and a celebration was held in honor of their victory.

After the feast was finished Gabriel soon start to prepare for their departure, "best of luck with your future adventures my friends, I hope that our paths will cross again someday" Boirin called out. Gabriel gave a happy chuckle and shouted, "I also hope that our paths will cross again, don't be a stranger. Feel free to visit my home whenever you wish."

After all of the good-byes were said Gabriel and his friends began to prepare for departure, Gabriel then looked toward the horizon and smiled. Soon the young Prince began to daydream about his homeland and his family, *"soon my adventures will and when they* are *over I will return to my beautiful Overon"* Gabriel thought happily.

Chapter Five

Obsession

As the young Elf-Prince and his companions prepared their supplies for departure, Kagan's older Brother Boirin hurried over to them and placed two large bags of jewels on one of their horses. "Consider this a reward for saving our people, young Elf-Prince" Boirin stated, Gabriel smiled happily and thanked the Dwarf warrior for his generosity.

Once all of their supplies were loaded the young Elf prepared for his journey homeward, as the days went by Gabriel's mind began to dwell on thoughts of his homeland. "I have been gone for so long, do you think that my parents may still remember my face?" questioned Gabriel; Vincent noticed the look of concern in Gabriel's and decided to cheer him up.

"Do not worry your highness, I am quite certain that your Mother and Father may still recognize you. I also believe that they will be very surprised to see the beautiful child that your wife has brought into the world" Vincent stated. After Vincent made his statement a smile immediately appeared on Gabriel's face and he then started to think of some beautiful memories of his home.

"*I can feel the sweet taste of the Baker's Berry Crumble Teacakes in my mouth already*" Gabriel thought happily, a few days went by and the warriors soon came across a divided path. "According to my map, the quickest way to Overon is to take the path through Greenwood Pass. That path will lead us to the kingdom of Stilwell, once we arrive there it's just a two day walk to Overon" Capt. Andromados said, Gabriel and his friends quickly agreed and began traveling down the path.

Soon the warriors' journey led them down a beautiful meadow and everything seemed oddly quiet at the time, suddenly a pack of glowing sparks appeared before them and they soon started firing smaller sparks at them. "What are these things and more importantly where the devil did they come from" Kagan grumbled while swinging his hands through the air, at that moment the sparks stopped firing all was quiet for the moment.

Suddenly all of the sparks started glowing brightly and the lights started to take form, when the lights faded Gabriel and his friends were soon surrounded by small winged creatures. "What are these things Gabriel?" Donella asked nervously, before Gabriel could answer his wife's question one of the creatures flew to his face and glared angrily at him.

"I am Princess Kendra, ruler of the Sprite kingdom of Sunniva and I will not allow any of you giant-folk to capture any more of my people" Kendra said angrily, Gabriel looked at his friends with concern and realized what Kendra was saying. "I assure you Princess Kendra, my friends and I are not giant-folk. My name is Gabriel and I am an Elf-Prince from the kingdom of Overon" Gabriel stated, Kendra still felt suspicious about Gabriel but when she took a closer look at him a smile soon appeared on her face.

"You speak the truth young Prince, I can see the truth in your eyes" Kendra said happily, after she became aquatinted with Gabriel Kendra was soon introduced to his friends and family. "It is a pleasure to meet all of you, I apologize for the actions of myself and my guards. We don't trust too many of the larger folk that come by here" Kendra stated.

Upon hearing the Princess' statement Donella looked at Kendra with concern and asked her why they don't trust many of the larger folk that pass her kingdom, "where exactly *is* your kingdom, if you don't mind me asking?" Catrina asked. Kendra then pointed her fingers downward and revealed to the company dozens of small buildings and houses (much like the size of dollhouses,) in the middle of this kingdom stood beautiful golden palace with tall towers and long banners waving in the wind.

"If that answers your question about my home I shall answer your other question, the reason my people have been living in fear for so long is because we have been repeatedly attacked by an Ogre named Sar" Kendra stated. Gabriel and Donella gave out loud gasps of horror and their son Avery whimpered loudly at the sound of the Ogre's name, "what would an Ogre want with Sprites, they may possess great magic but I doubt that an *Ogre* would know of such things" questioned Kagan.

"No one knows, he just keeps returning to my home time-after-time and capturing more and more of my people every time" Kendra said sadly, at that moment a young Knight stepped forward. The Knight had long black hair, black eyes a handsome face and was dressed in the finest suit of armor ever made; "do not despair your highness, somehow we will find a way to rescue our captured comrades" the Knight said reassuringly.

Kendra looked at the Knight with tearstained eyes and smiled, soon another Sprite appeared and she placed her hand on Kendra's shoulder for comfort. "List is right my dear, the rest of our people will return. I promise you that" the female stated, Gabriel looked at Kendra with concern and asked her who her friends were. "This is Whitney, she has been my dearest friend for many years and she is also the most trusted member of my court" Kendra said while introducing her friend, she then turned to the young Knight and blushed a deep shade of red.

"This young gentleman is List, he is one of my royal Knights and he and ever since Sar first attacked us he has hardly ever left my side ever since" Kendra giggled, Donella and the others looked at each other with concern while Gabriel gave Kendra an inquisitive stare. *"Methinks that there is something more going on between Kendra and this young Knight"* Gabriel thought, after everything was explained Gabriel and his friends agreed to go find the other members of Kendra's people.

Moments later Gabriel and his companions gathered up their supplies and journeyed toward the one place where they would find the Ogre, the Swamp of Shadows. When they arrived they were soon assaulted by the foulest odor they have ever smelled, "ugh, the Ogre must be here. Only an Ogre can give out a stench *this* foul" Kagan grumbled.

As the team began to journey across the swamp they soon heard loud laughing noises in the distance, *"ha-ha-ha, Sar love shiny things. Pretty shiny things make Sar happy"* a voice laughed loudly. Gabriel and his friends traveled deep into the swamp till finally they found the source, standing before them was a huge Ogre with repulsive green skin, dressed in a cloak made of fur, a huge brown nose, shaggy, black hair, and huge pink eyes.

The Ogre then stared at a small jar and started to laugh again, when Gabriel took a closer look at the jar he saw a small creature flying frantically around it. "That must be one of the Sprites that was captured from Sunniva, she seems all right for now but what does the Ogre want with them" Gabriel whispered, suddenly Avery's nose started to twitch and soon he prepared to sneeze.

Donella tried to keep her child from sneezing but failed, Avery let a small but otherwise loud sneeze and the sound soon reached the Ogre's ears. The Ogre then started to sniff the air repeatedly till he finally turned his head in Gabriel's direction, "Sar smell baddies, baddies try to take shiny things away from Sar. Sar crush baddies" Sar growled.

The Ogre then jumped to his feet and raced toward the shore, as the Ogre neared closer to them Gabriel and his friends prepared for battle. "My friend, I don't mean any disrespect but I must ask you to release those creatures" Gabriel commanded, the Ogre growled loudly and began to swing his club rapidly in the air. "Sar won't let you take his shiny things, Sar will crush you" Sar shouted, at that moment Kendra appeared before Sar and glared at him angrily.

"Those are not 'shiny things' as you call them, those are my people and I order you to release them at once" Kendra demanded, Sar gave a low growl and snatched Kendra in his massive green hands. Kendra tried to break free of the Sar's grasp but his grip was too tight for her to break free, things seemed utterly hopeless for the young Sprite as the Ogre began to slowly squeeze the life out of her.

Suddenly Sar felt a sharp jolt of pain surge through his hand and lost his grip on Kendra, "ouch, that hurt. Who hit me?" Sar demanded. As Sar began to lick his wound angrily the young Knight named List soon appeared, "I will not let you harm one hair on Kendra's head, if you wish to harm her you will have to plow through me first" List stated.

Sar gave an angry snarl and charged toward List with his club high in the air, while the Ogre was distracted Gabriel and his friends raced toward the jars that contained the rest of Kendra's people. "Do not be afraid everyone, my friends and I are here to rescue you" Gabriel explained to the other Sprites, the creatures seemed alarmed by the size of Gabriel and his friends but when the jar lids were loosened their fears soon disappeared.

"Many thanks to you young Elf for rescuing us, now we must aid the Princess at once" one Sprite stated, after all of the Sprites said their thanks they grabbed their weapons and prepared to do battle with Sar. Despite the Ogre's great size he was still unable to overpower all of the

Sprites that flew around him, "keep fighting everyone, do not let him escape our fury" Kendra commanded.

As the Sprites continued to fight Gabriel noticed something very odd, soon a small tear appeared underneath Sar's right eye and soon the Ogre started to cry. "Hold, everyone hold. Lower your arms at once" Gabriel begged; Kendra and the other members of her kingdom looked at the Elf-Prince with concern and asked him why should lower their arms, "the Ogre is crying, he is scared of you. I do not think he wants to fight us" Gabriel stated.

When the Sprites lowered their weapons Princess Kendra flew over to Sar and placed her hand on his head, "calm yourself Sar, we will not hurt you again. But if you try to hurt my people again I will have no choice but to do so" Kendra said calmly. Sar slowly lifted his and dried away his tears before speaking to the Princess, "Sar no hurt you, Sar love shiny things. Sar saw something glowing in meadows, Sar did not mean to hurt you" Sar said between sniffles.

After hearing Sar's statement he asked Catrina to hand him the sacks of jewels they received from Kagan's Cousin Boirin, "Sar, look here. Look at all of these pretty stones we have, if you set the Sprites free we will give you all of these stones" Gabriel offered. When the Ogre saw the jewels glowing in the bag his eyes brightened up with happiness, "ooh, shiny rocks. Sar love shiny rocks, thank you tiny Elf" Sar said happily.

Gabriel gave a bright smile and handed Sar the biggest sack of jewels they had, after all of the jewels were given Sar hurried over and released the remaining Sprites from their jars. After the situation with Sar was settled Gabriel and his friends escorted the Sprites back to the Sunniva, "many thanks to you my friends, not only did you rescue my people but you also helped us gain a new friend as well" Kendra stated.

Gabriel gave a big smile and bowed his head; his friend soon did the same and once all of the thanks were said Kendra asked a few of her servants to bring something forward. Once the command was made four of Kendra's servant hurried into the treasury room and returned with a beautiful golden medallion in their hands.

"This is the Medallion of Foster, with it you can possess the power of Psychic Ability and speak to other creatures of the world with your mind. Use it well my fiends and I hope we will meet again someday" Kendra said with a smile, Gabriel bowed his head in thanks and prepared for departure. Before they left Donella walked over to Kendra and asked her where the quickest path back to Overon was, "the best path to take to Overon would be through the city of Seber, it lies in to the East. Once you pass through there you must pass through the kingdom of Stilwell and once you do you will see your home again" Kendra explained.

Donella thanked Kendra for her instructions and began her preparations for departure, "before you all leave there is something you should know, once you arrive in Stilwell do not look for welcome there. A dark presence now looms over the royal family and all that was once good there is now slowly disappearing" Kendra said sadly. Hearing this new sent an icy chill down Gabriel's spine.

"A dark presence in Stilwell, that is where Cedric lives. I hope he is alright" Gabriel thought, Mako's cousin Shegra soon noticed the look of fear in Gabriel's eyes and decided to cheer him up. "What is the matter Gabriel, you're awfully quiet?" Shegra asked with concern, Gabriel quickly shook of his fear and told her that he would explain everything later on.

After he carefully placed the medallion in his pouch Gabriel and his friends took one last look at the Sprite kingdom and began to journey toward the East. Meanwhile in the kingdom of Overon, a dark figure sat on his throne looking into a magical projection of the Greenwood Pass.

"I'm looking forward to your arrival my old friend, I have big plans for you" the figure said in a deep voice, the figure then waved his hand over the looking glass and laughed loudly. "Once I gather my forces together not even you will be able to stop me" the figure said while looking into another projection, the figure then commanded his guards to hurry off to the outskirts of the kingdom to prepare for the young Elf-Prince's arrival.

CHAPTER SIX

Behind the Curtain

Many weeks passed by since Gabriel and his friends left the Sprite kingdom of Sunniva and in time things quickly became dire for the brave warriors; soon they found themselves low on supplies and some members of the company began to grow weary. "If we do not find food or water soon I'll collapse right on the spot" Kagan grumbled, the other warriors silently grumbled as Mako began to search the pouches on one of the horses for what little scraps of food they had left.

"I cannot move an inch more, I must find some water or I will surely die of thirst" Catrina cried, while the others complained about their hunger and thirst Gabriel soon spotted some firelight in the distance. "Friends, I see firelight straight ahead. There might be a camp nearby, we must make haste" Gabriel stated, the warriors gathered what little strength they had left and hurried behind Gabriel.

After ten minutes of running Gabriel and his friends soon found the source of the firelight, it turned out to be chimney smoke coming from a house in the middle of a huge village. "Where the devil are we?" questioned Kagan, Vincent turned to his side and spotted a large wooden sign waving in the wind that said "Welcome to Seber."

"According to the sign, this is the kingdom of Seber" Vincent stated, after Vincent made his statement Gabriel's heart was quickly filled with joy. "Once we pass through this city it's only a matter of time before we reach Overon" Gabriel said happily, at that moment Gabriel felt a light tug on the edge of his cloak and looked down to see his infant son with a sad look in his eyes.

"I want to return to Overon as much as you do my dear, but we must first rest ourselves or we will never make it home" Donella said sincerely, suddenly Gabriel heard a low grumbling sound and soon realized that it was his stomach calling out to him. "I guess we all could use a little refueling, I see an Inn nearby. Follow me everyone" Gabriel suggested while point to his right, once they entered the Inn Gabriel and his friends were welcomed with open arms by the Innkeeper.

"Welcome to my humble inn, if you should ever need anything I shall be there to answer your calls" the Innkeeper said happily, moments later the young warriors were fed and were given all of the care they needed. "Thank you for your hospitality my friend, here is your payment. I hope it will be enough" Donella said while handing the Innkeeper a pouch of gold coins, as he began to prepare his supplies for departure Gabriel spotted a poster with a young gentleman on it with short brown hair, black eyes and a small beard wearing a Violet cape.

"Tell me, Innkeeper. Who is this young man and why is a poster of him plastered on your wall?" Gabriel asked the Innkeeper, "that is Clortho, he is a Mage who possesses the power to control every beast ever known. He is the greatest Beast-Master in the entire kingdom and tomorrow he is going to perform in the Town-Square" the Innkeeper explained. Gabriel became instantly amazed the Mage's great reputation but soon remembered that he had to return to his home at once, Donella quickly saw the tense look in Gabriel's eyes and decided to cheer him up by placing her hand on his shoulder.

"Let's stay here for a little while longer Gabriel, we have been traveling for months and I have a feeling that you could use a little relaxation"

Donella begged, Gabriel felt a little unsure at the moment but when he saw the pleading look in his wife's eyes he smiled. "Very well, we shall stay here and rest. This 'Beast-Master' sounds like an interesting fellow" Gabriel laughed, once the agreement was made Gabriel hurried up the stairs and drifted off into a deep slumber.

The next mourning everyone from all over the kingdom gathered at the Town-Square to see the mysterious Clortho, during the show Clortho commanded a huge Manticore to do amazing aerial stunts and the entire audience gasped with amazement. During another segment of the show Clortho trained a Griffin to sing a beautiful song and the crowd began to clap their hands loudly, as the show quickly drew to an end Clortho faced the crowd and began to make an announcement.

"I am pleased that you are enjoying the show so far my friends, now the time has come for our finale. For my final performance of the evening I am going to ask for the aid of a lovely young maiden, with her help we shall see if music can truly charm the savage beast" Clortho stated while revealing a giant Basilisk. When the beast saw the crowd it let out a loud hiss and started to lick its lips loudly with hunger, seeing this made the entire crowd (including Gabriel and his companions) gasp in horror.

"Do not fear, as long as I hold this staff no beast shall ever harm you" Clortho said reassuringly, suddenly Clortho waved his hands and a huge puff of smoke appeared on the stage. When the smoke cleared away a beautiful young woman soon came into view, she had long red hair, black eyes, lightly tanned skin and a beautiful gold-colored dress.

The crowd soon started doubting Clortho and started to lose confidence in him, "I can see the look of doubt in your eyes my friends, but I assure you there is nothing to worry about. So please join me in welcoming my lovely assistant, Hilda" Clortho announced. As the crowd silenced themselves Hilda took a deep breath and began to sing in a beautiful Elvish language, the song sounded so wonderful that the Basilisk soon started to fall asleep.

When the young lady's performance came to an end the Town-Square echoed with the loud sounds of cheering and applause, moments later Clortho and his fellow performers packed up their equipment and prepared to leave the Town-Square when they were suddenly delayed by Gabriel and his friends. "Master Clortho, I apologize for disturbing you and your fellow performers. But I just had to come and congratulate you on such an excellent performance" Gabriel said with happiness.

Clortho gave an appreciative smile and bowed his head; "I appreciate your opinion my young friend, I am glad that you and your friends enjoyed the show" Clortho stated, he then turned toward his friends and introduced them to Gabriel. "This is young chap is Malcolm, he is one of my assistants" Clortho said while pointing to a young man with short black hair and an angry look in his eyes.

Clortho then faced the young lady and soon felt a light blush develop on his face, "this is Hilda, she has been a great help in many of my performances. There are certain creatures in this world that can't be tamed by my magic alone" Clortho explained, Hilda gave a smile and bowed her head to Gabriel and his friends.

After all of the introductions were said Clortho journeyed back to the Inn with the young Prince for a well-deserved rest, when the sun finally set all of the people of Seber soon drifted of to a deep sleep. Suddenly Gabriel's sharp ears picked up a sound from outside of the Inn; he got up from his bed and tiptoed over to the window to find a very surprising site, standing outside of the Inn was a hooded figure with a baby Griffin at his side.

The figure then snapped his fingers and the Griffin quietly flew through the window of a nearby building, Gabriel was a little suspicious at first but then started to think that it wasn't too serious and so he went back to sleep. The next morning after they had a warm breakfast Gabriel and his friends packed up their bags for departure, as they exited the Inn the company spotted a large crowd forming in front of a large building at the edge of town.

Gabriel raced over and asked one of villagers what the problem was, "there was a robbery here in the treasury last night, the guards said that a hooded figure holding a red staff passed by here. The next thing they saw was a flock of baby Griffins flying out of the building with huge sacks of gold in their mouths" the man explained.

Gabriel wondered why a flock of Griffins had sacks of gold in their mouths and why someone other than Clortho would have a red staff, suddenly the young Elf-Prince heard sounds of struggling coming from the back of the crowd and he quickly raced to the source. When he arrived at the scene Gabriel saw two guards from the royal army holding Clortho in chains, "back away everyone, this man is a thief and he will be punished severely for his crimes" the guard shouted.

"What sort of crimes has this man committed sir?" questioned Gabriel, the guard told the crowd that Clortho was accused of using his magic to steal the money from the treasury and pointed out that they also found one of the stolen rubies in Clortho's bedroom. Gabriel's eyes grew wide with shock and he tried to convince the guard that Clortho was innocent, "I admire your spirit master Elf but all of the evidence points to Clortho, not only that but one of Clortho's assistants said that he saw him near the treasury" the guard explained.

Gabriel tried to defend Clortho once more but the guard silenced him before he could say one word, "please sir, I assure you that this is all a huge misunderstanding. Please allow me to try and prove Clortho's innocence" Gabriel begged. The guard scratched his chin for a few seconds till finally he gave a nod and gave Gabriel permission to help clear Clortho's name, once that was settled Gabriel and his friends hurried over to Clortho's bedroom to try and find some clues.

"This is like trying to find a needle in a haystack, we've been searching this room for five hours now" Kagan grumbled, even though Gabriel did not agree with Kagan's enthusiasm he soon started to lose hope as well. Suddenly Avery looked over his mother's shoulder and started cooing very loudly; Donella turned to her son and wondered why he was making so much noise, she then looked down and saw a line a footprints leading toward the windowsill.

Donella took a closer look at the footprints and noticed that they were still fresh, "these footprints must belong to the person who framed Clortho, I wish we could find some more clues" Donella stated. As the warriors continued searching the room Catrina spotted a trunk sitting near a bed, she took a closer look at the trunk and noticed that it was unlocked and a piece of brown cloth was caught in the lock.

When she called the others over to the trunk Catrina showed them all of the clues she found, *"this cloth seems very familiar, I feel like I've seen it before"* Gabriel thought. He then remembered that when he saw Clortho at the show one of his assistants had a piece of cloth missing from his right sleeve, then at that moment the truth quickly hit him like a flash.

"I know who committed all of these crimes, we must return to the Town-Square immediately" Gabriel instructed while gathering all of the pieces of evidence together, meanwhile at the Town-Square the royal guards and all of the villagers gathered together to watch Clortho's trial. "Before we sentence you to your punishment Clortho I would just like to say that you should be ashamed of yourself for using your magic skills for stealing" the Captain of the guard said sadly, Clortho tried to defend himself but he was immediately silenced by the Captain's troops.

"For stealing from the city treasury, you are here by sentenced to be hanged from the highest gallows" the Captain announced, once the trail was finished the royal guards escorted Clortho to the gallows where he was to be hanged. Once they took Clortho to the top of the steps the Captain began to tie the noose tightly around Clortho's neck; after the noose was tightened one of the Captain's troops prepared to open the trap door when suddenly Gabriel raced forward and stopped him.

"Halt, set this man free at once. We have found out who the real criminal is" Gabriel stated, the townspeople all looked at Gabriel with concern and they all started wondering if he was just stalling for time so Clortho could escape. Gabriel then asked Kagan and Mako to bring over the trunk that contained Clortho's equipment, "while my friends and I were searching for clues we found a collection of footprints leading toward the window that faced the treasury, we also noticed that Clortho's trunk was mysteriously unlocked" Gabriel explained.

He then reached into his pocket and pulled out the piece of brown cloth that he found in the trunk, when Malcolm saw the color of the cloth he became very nervous. "We also found this small piece of cloth wedged inside the trunk, whoever tried to take Clortho's staff must have caused the lid to accidentally close on their shirtsleeve" Gabriel stated.

As Gabriel continued with his explanation he soon noticed that Malcolm started becoming more and more nervous by the minute, he walked over to him and gave the young performer a concerned stare. "Why are you so nervous my friend, you don't have anything to hide. Do you?" questioned Gabriel, soon Malcolm started to shake as if it was the middle of winter and that gave Gabriel all the proof he needed.

Before Malcolm could say one word Gabriel lifted the performers right arm and saw a small hole underneath his sleeve, "just as I thought, it was *you* who robbed the treasury not Clortho. Only one question remains, why would you try to frame Clortho when he has done nothing harmful against you?" Gabriel asked. Malcolm gave a low growl and raced away from the crowd, "I shall tell you why I did it, I am the one who truly deserves everything Clortho has. His mastery over beasts, all his wealth and the admiration of the beautiful Hilda" Malcolm shouted.

After hearing Malcolm's statement the entire crowd looked at him with shock and disgust, "men, release Clortho from his shackles. I'll deal with Malcolm" the Captain of the guard commanded, to the guards dismay Malcolm quickly snatched away Clortho's staff before they could capture him. Malcolm then held the staff high above his head and summoned a giant Manticore to his aid, "now *I* am the Beast-Master fools, I may have failed to rid myself of Clortho but I can still take what is rightfully mine" Malcolm proclaimed.

When the creature arrived at the Town-Square Malcolm snapped his fingers and the Manticore quickly snatched Hilda into its huge talons, "Hilda, no. We have to save her" Clortho stated. The Manticore continued to fly higher and higher into the air with Hilda screaming fearfully in its claws, while Clortho tried to think of a way to get his staff back Gabriel soon came up with a solution.

The young Elf pulled out a small boomerang from his pouch and threw it toward Malcolm's hand, when the boomerang finally hit it's target Malcolm grabbed his hand in pain and the staff fell to the ground. When the staff fell the Manticore stopped in midair and moved his head around in confusion, as the Manticore tried to figure out what was going on its grip on Hilda began to loosen.

At that moment the Manticore's claws completely lost their grip around the young maiden and she began to fall faster and faster to the ground below her, thinking quickly Clortho grabbed his staff and began chanting an incantation. After the incantation was recited a magical energy force immediately caught Hilda; after Hilda was safely lowered to the ground the Manticore flew over to Clortho and gave everyone a confused stare, when the Manticore saw Clortho it nudged its head on him playfully.

"It's good to see you old friend, now I must take care of a little problem" Clortho stated, before Clortho could say one word Malcolm began to race through the crowd like a mad man. While the royal guards chased after Malcolm Clortho raised his staff in the air and captured Malcolm with the same spell he used to save Hilda, after Malcolm was taken in by the guards all of the gold and jewels were returned to the their proper place in the treasury.

"We apologize for our behavior Clortho, can you ever forgive us?" the Captain begged, Clortho gave a smile and assured the people that he didn't hold any grudges. As Clortho continued speaking to the crowd Hilda quietly walked over to him and tapped him on the shoulder, "I just wanted to thank you for saving my life Clortho, I don't know how I'll be able to repay you" Hilda said blushing.

"There's no need to thank me, when someone you care about is in danger you have to help them no matter what the cost" Clortho stated, Hilda smiled happily and decided to thank Clortho in the best way she could. Before Clortho could react Hilda leaned in and kissed his lips, the kiss lasted for a few seconds till finally their lung's demand for air finally ended it.

When the kiss ended Gabriel and his friends all gave him a sly stare, after Clortho helped Hilda get back on her feet he thanked Gabriel and his companions for clearing his name and they all said their good-byes. "Good luck on the rest of your journey Gabriel and perhaps one day we will meet again" Clortho said with a smile, as the young Prince and his companions began to leave the kingdom the townspeople all waved good-bye and shouted their thanks to them.

After they left the kingdom the company was more then ready for the next part of their adventure, "I cannot wait till we arrive in Stilwell, I'm looking forward to introducing you all to my old friend Cedric" Gabriel said happily. As the warriors began to leave the sight of the kingdom of Seber Gabriel soon felt a chill down his spine; "Is something the matter Gabriel?" Donella asked with concern, Gabriel shook his head and told his wife not to worry.

Donella couldn't help but think that Gabriel was something from her, suddenly Donella felt the same chill that Gabriel felt run down her spine. *"That must have been what Gabriel felt, I can sense a dark presence in the air as we draw nearer to Stilwell. I fear that we won't be so warmly welcomed as Gabriel believes"* Donella thought sadly.

CHAPTER SEVEN

Bitter Reunions

As the company began to journey toward the kingdom of Stilwell Gabriel smiled happily and began to think of how wonderful it would be to see his old friend again, *"it's been may long years since I've traveled this road, I hope Cedric and his family are well"* Gabriel thought. While the others were at the campsite preparing a meal Kagan raced to the top of a nearby hill to see if they were getting close to Stilwell, when Kagan arrived at the top of the hill he saw a band of horsemen racing toward their campsite.

"Those horsemen seem to be running from something but I do not see anything chasing them" Kagan said curiously, he then called everyone to the top of hill and showed them the frightened horsemen. Gabriel took a closer look at the riders and noticed that one of them was carrying a flag with the Stilwell royal crest on it, as the riders drew nearer to them Gabriel quickly signaled them to stop.

"What business brings you and your friends to the kingdom of Stilwell, master Elf?" one rider demanded, "I am Prince Gabriel of Overon, I am journeying toward Stilwell to see Prince Cedric" Gabriel stated. When Gabriel mentioned the name Cedric the guard lowered his head and told the warriors they were trying to escape the kingdom, "why the devil would you try to escape from your own home?" questioned Kagan.

Suddenly a loud scream echoed through the air and caused all of their horses to whinny very loudly, "*that* is why we are fleeing from here, our people have been suffering for many days at the hands of our young Prince. No one knows why he is behaving this way but if anyone dared to question him they would be severely punished" the guard explained. After hearing the guard's statement Gabriel looked at him with disbelief, "that is preposterous, Cedric is the kindest person I have ever met. He wouldn't harm a fly" Gabriel said with disbelief.

After seeing the look of determination in Gabriel's eyes the guards had no choice but to let them pass through, "word of advice young Elf; when you arrive at the palace, do not look for welcome there" the guard stated. When Gabriel and his friends arrived in the village all of the townspeople looked at them with fear, "I've seen graveyards more lively than this place" Kagan grumbled.

When they reached the royal palace Donella and the others started to feel an odd presence from somewhere; Gabriel however ignored the feeling and happily knocked on the gate. When they were given permission to enter Gabriel quickly raced inward to see his friend, when he arrived inside the Throne Room Gabriel was in for a hideous surprise. The person sitting on the throne was Cedric but he had pale-white skin, long and shaggy white hair, ripped clothes and a tired look in his eyes.

Seeing one of his dearest friends in such a horrible state sent a chill down his spine, before his friends could utter one word Gabriel quickly raced to the throne and placed his hand on Cedric's shoulder. "Cedric my friend, what has happened to you" Gabriel asked with concern, after hearing the young Elf's voice Cedric began to slowly lift his head and open his eyes.

When Gabriel's image finally came clear to Cedric's eyes a smile slowly developed on his face, "Gabriel, my dear old friend. It's good to see you again after so long" Cedric said in a raspy voice. After hearing the odd sound in Cedric's voice Gabriel asked him for an explanation, "I'm afraid much has changed since the last time you were here Gabriel, an evil Mage named Brogan attacked the kingdom long ago and destroyed our noblest of warriors" Cedric explained.

Gabriel looked at Cedric with sadness in his eyes and tried to think of a way to help him, suddenly he heard a faint cry for help from somewhere in the room and tried to find the source. Since Gabriel's Elf-ears had a sharper sense of hearing than that of most creatures he could easily hear any sound no matter how soft it was, Gabriel's eyes searched every corner of the Throne Room till finally he found the source of the sound.

Gabriel looked down at Cedric's right hand and spotted a ring with a large Sapphire stone on it glowing brightly, *"how odd, I have never seen Cedric wear that ring before. I wonder where he got it?"* Gabriel asked himself. He drew his gaze back up to Cedric's eyes and prepared to question him about the ring when suddenly Cedric quickly broke the silence, "you like it, this ring is like no other type of jewelry in the world. I found it after Brogan's first arrival" Cedric stated.

Everyone in the room gave Cedric a concerned stare and began to whisper to each other in fear, "I have an ill about that ring, I think it would be wise to rid yourself of it while you can milord" Kagan requested. While he was listening to Kagan's request Cedric started to hear voices, *"beware Cedric, do not trust the outsiders. They will bring harm upon you and seize your throne"* an eerie voice stated.

To everyone's surprise Cedric gave out a horrified gasp and he nearly jumped out of his throne in fear, "Cedric, are you alright. Let me help you to your bed chambers" Gabriel said sincerely while offering his hand to Cedric. Suddenly Cedric swatted Gabriel's hand away and pulled out his sword, "away with you, vile wretches. I will not let you take my kingdom" Cedric shouted.

Gabriel tried to convince Cedric that he was only trying to help him to bed, unfortunately the young Elf-Prince's attempts were in vain as Cedric prepared to summon his guards. "Guards, capture them at once!" Cedric commanded, before the guards could capture them a small stone slab on the floor began to move and a hooded figure soon appeared from below.

"Climb down here young Elf, I will take you to safety" the figure stated, even though he was unsure about trusting the woman Gabriel had no choice but to follow her. Once Gabriel and his friends escaped through the secret passage they followed the stranger through a dark and dank underground maze, "I don't think we should be here, I don't trust this hooded stranger" Kagan stated.

At that moment the stranger stopped walking and faced the Dwarf with a very serious look in her eyes, she then reached up for the back of her cloak and gently removed it to reveal her true self. She was a young and beautiful woman with short, brown hair, blue eyes and baby-soft skin. She wore a beautiful yellow gown and wore beautiful jewelry on her fingers and neck.

"You wish to know if you can trust me, very well. I am Edith, Queen of Stilwell and I apologize for my son's actions. After he defeated Brogan he has been acting very strangely ever since, but I know that some amount of goodness still remains within him" Edith said with hope in her voice. She then led the Elf-Prince and his friends to a secret room filled with some of the villagers and a few members of the kingdom's royal court, once Edith took her companions inside the room everyone looked at them with shock and concern.

"Edith, what are you doing bringing outsiders here. They could put us all in jeopardy and have us all tossed into the castle dungeons" a tall man shouted, when Gabriel heard the sound of the man's voice he felt joy fill up inside him. Before Gabriel could say anything to the man Kagan stepped forward and glared at him, "mind your tongue old fool, this is Gabriel of Overon. I believe that he was one of your son's friends" Kagan growled.

After Gabriel's identity was revealed the tall man stepped forward and took a closer look at the Prince, after studying the young Elf's appearance for ten seconds the man smiled and began to laugh loudly. "So the Dwarf speaks the truth, you *are* Prince Gabriel. Look how you've grown, when last I looked you were but a small child" the man said happily, Gabriel gave a smile and happily embraced the tall man.

Capt. Andromados slowly walked over to Gabriel and asked him how he knew the strangers, Gabriel then realized that proper introductions were needed at the moment. "This is Queen Edith and her husband King Valarian. He and his wife have been loyal friends and allies with my family for many years" Gabriel stated, after all of the introductions were finished King Valarian and Queen Edith sat Gabriel and his friends down for Supper. During the meal Gabriel and his friends told the King and Queen about all of the adventures they've had up till their arrival in Stillwell, "what a wonderful story Gabriel, it looks as if we aren't the only ones who have suffered" King Valarian said sadly.

"What happened your highness, Stilwell was so beautiful when I came here long ago" Gabriel said with concern, King Valarian gave a deep sigh and began his tale. "Three years ago we were ruthlessly attacked by a Mage named Brogan, he lived in a dark citadel somewhere in the mountains and experimented with Dark Magic of every sort.

One day he stumbled upon a spell that would give him the ability to absorb the souls of every warrior or creature he vanquished, but in order to use this power Brogan needed a vessel to place the power in. No one truly knows what type of vessel Brogan chose to hold the power in but many of us believe that he used a ring he wore around his finger, after he placed the magic inside the ring Brogan began to unleash its power upon our people" King Valarian explained.

After hearing half of the tale Gabriel and his companions became both frightened and worried about Cedric, "I do not mean any disrespect Valarian but how does this incident involve your son?" Mako asked. The King gave another deep sigh and continued his tale, "as Brogan continued to attack our kingdom my son Cedric brought it upon himself to strike him down, when Cedric arrived on the battlefield he glared at the Mage and demanded Brogan to leave kingdom at once.

In response to Cedric's demands Brogan pulled out his sword and attacked my son with every ounce of strength he possessed, the battle ragged on for what seemed like an eternity till finally Cedric picked up a mace and swung it with all his might. The mace delivered a powerful blow to the Mage's chest and he was quickly struck down, as Brogan began to stand back on his feet he quickly noticed that he was low on strength and had no choice but to retreat" Valarian stated.

After King Valarian's story was done Gabriel gave his friends a very concerned stare; *"I still don't understand why Cedric is behaving so strangely, could it involve the Mage somehow?"* Gabriel thought, "do you believe that there is a connection between Brogan's attack and Cedric's strange behavior?" questioned Gabriel. *"You are correct Master Gabriel, there* is *a connection between the battle and the Prince's behavior"* a voice called out, upon hearing the voice Gabriel and his friends turned their heads to find a young Princess and a young man standing behind them.

The young maiden had a pair of violet colored eyes, skin as smooth and pale as the snow and she wore a beautiful violet-blue dress with long black gloves. She wore a small golden bracelet on her wrist, her raven-black hair was tied into a long ponytail that reached below her waist and she wore a long, golden necklace around her neck.

The person standing next to the Princess was a tan-skinned lad with long, black hair, black eyes, a golden suit of armor and a shield with the image of a Silver bird on it. "Amelia, bless you child you're safe, did anyone see you?" Edith asked fearfully, Amelia gave a smile and assured the Queen that none of the guards saw her moving around the palace.

"I felt frightened at first and thought that Cedric's guards would immediately spot me, but Paige provided excellent protection for me my Queen" Amelia said reassuringly, King Valarian turned toward the Elf- Prince and introduced the young maiden. "This lovely young lass is Princess Amelia, She's my son's wife but ever since he changed Cedric turned his back on her as well as the kingdom" the King said sadly, Gabriel then noticed the Princess rubbing her stomach repeatedly.

"Is something troubling you milady?" Gabriel asked with concern, Amelia gave a chuckle and told Gabriel and his friends that she about to have a baby. "A baby, splendid news milady. Does your husband know of this?" Shegra asked, "yes, Cedric does know about the baby. But ever since he found that accursed ring Cedric has forgotten about the joy of having a family" Amelia said sadly.

Upon hearing Amelia's statement Valarian finally solved the mystery, "so it's true, that ring *is* the cause of all this. That must have been the ring that Brogan dropped after he was struck down" Valarian stated. "You may be right sire, before your wife led me and my friends here I heard faint cries for help coming from a ring on Cedric's right hand. If we can just get the ring off of Cedric he may be able to return to normal" the young Prince stated.

As Gabriel continued to explain his plan loud rumbling sounds suddenly echoed throughout the room, hearing these sounds caused all of the people in the room to whimper in fear. When the rumbling stopped all was quiet at the moment until a dozen of Cedric's royal knights charged in, "it's just as you suspected sire, the rebels and your parents *have* been hiding under the palace" one guard shouted.

"Restrain them at once, all except the Elf. I wish to handle him myself" Cedric said with a snicker, without a moment's hesitation the guards grabbed a dozen long coils of chains and wrapped it tightly around all of the rebels while leaving Gabriel untouched. "This is quite a surprise Gabriel, seeing you among the rebels. I thought you and I were friends" Cedric said coldly, "the *real* Cedric and I *are* friends, but you are not him. That ring your wearing has corrupted your mind and turned you into some sort of monster" Gabriel shouted angrily.

Cedric walked over to the young Elf and gave him an ice-cold glare, "you dare to question my power, I believe the time has come for someone to put you in your place Elf. Guards, escort Gabriel to the Courtyard" Cedric command. Moments later Gabriel, Cedric and all of the citizens of Stilwell gathered at the battlefield to watch the two Princes fight to the death.

"Do you remember this place Gabriel, this is where we used to play together when we were young. This shall be the perfect place for everyone to witness your ultimate downfall" Cedric laughed, the crowd remained silent as Gabriel and Cedric began to ready themselves for battle. King Valarian slowly stepped off his seat and reluctantly gave the signal to commence the battle.

After the signal was given Cedric held his sword high in the air, gave a loud roar and charged toward Gabriel like a madman, thinking quickly Gabriel removed his cape and used it to pull Cedric's sword from his hands. After reclaiming his sword Cedric became very enraged and tried many times to strike Gabriel down, unfortunately Cedric was so overcome with rage that he failed every strike.

"What is the meaning of this Gabriel, cease this behavior and fight me" Cedric growled, Gabriel sadly lowered his head, gave a deep sigh and dropped his sword to the ground. "No Cedric, you and I have been friends for many years. I will never harm you no matter what" Gabriel said with tears forming in his eyes, as Gabriel fell to his knees crying it gave Cedric the opportunity to deliver one final blow.

"Strike me if you must, but I will not fight you. I know that signs of my old friend still remain deep within you" Gabriel said while looking up at Cedric, suddenly Cedric's arms froze in midair and his whole body went stiff. He then dropped his sword and looked at Gabriel with a shocked expression on his face, seeing Cedric drop his guard so quickly made Gabriel feel very concerned.

"Are you feeling ill Cedric, please let me help you" Gabriel pleaded, while Gabriel tried to aid his friend many people from the crowd looked at each other and started whispering questionably. "What the devil is going on, is Cedric hurt?" questioned King Valarian, the King then commanded Paige to rush to Cedric's aid immediately.

Suddenly to everyone's surprise a tall figure dressed in a dark hooded cloak raced into the battlefield, the figure had pale-white skin, a long pointed beard and bright-red eyes. The figure then pushed Gabriel aside with his magic and he then turned his attention toward Cedric, "I believe that you have something of mine young one" the figure said harshly.

The figure then began reaching toward Cedric's hand and started smiling fiendishly, after seeing the look of evil in the man's eyes Cedric immediately pulled his hand away. "I don't know who you are, but I will not let you have this ring" Cedric shouted, Gabriel and his friends in the crowd could not figure out why the stranger was so interested in Cedric's ring until King Valarian figured out why.

"That's Brogan, the Mage has returned" Valarian shouted, after hearing the King's fearful cries the Mage turned to face him and laughed evilly. "Aye sire, I *am* Brogan. The same Mage that ravaged your land long ago and I have come back to reclaim what I have lost" Brogan chuckled, he then tackled Cedric and started pulling his finger.

"Get off of my friend you cur" Gabriel growled while pulling at his cape, Brogan gave a low growl and used a small portion of his magic to force Gabriel off of his back. "Stand aside Elf, the Prince stole my ring from me and I intend to get it back. By any means necessary" Brogan proclaimed; the Mage then conjured up every ounce of strength he had within him for one more tug.

Brogan pulled and pulled with all his might till finally a loud "CRACK" echoed through the skies, the crowd, the King and Queen looked on in horror as Brogan held up Cedric's finger and began laughing fiendishly. After Brogan's deed was finished he tossed Cedric aside and left him wincing and crying in pain, upon seeing her beloved in so much pain Princess Amelia immediately began to rush to his aid.

As Amelia prepared to jump over the barrier she suddenly felt a twitch in her stomach and collapsed, "oh my word, Amelia are you alright?" Edith asked fearfully. Amelia grabbed her stomach in pain and demanded that someone help her immediately, "my Queen, it's time" Amelia said painfully.

Queen Edith quickly understood what Amelia was saying and commanded the guards to escort her into the palace, after the Princess was taken to safety Queen Edith quickly raced to her son's aid. When she arrived at Cedric's side her eyes soon beheld an amazing miracle; Cedric's body soon began an amazing transformation, first his hair color changed back from Grey to Black and finally his skin quickly returned to its youthful sheen.

"At last, the Ring of Souls is where it belongs" Brogan yelled proudly, after he removed the ring from Cedric's dismembered finger Brogan threw the finger to the ground and placed the ring back on his hand. "Now that my ring is back on my hand I can now punish the one who stole it from me" he said while glaring at Cedric, Brogan then lifted his sword high up in the air and prepared to deliver the final blow to Cedric.

Suddenly Gabriel quickly raced up to Brogan from behind and stabbed him in the back with his blade; the Mage let out a loud, agonizing scream as Gabriel continued to plunge his sword deeper and deeper into his chest. "Do you feel that you accursed fiend, that is the same pain that your ring caused all of these people and I'm going to see to it that it doesn't happen again" Gabriel snarled, Brogan tried many attempts to push Gabriel off of him but failed every time.

Finally after what seemed like an eternity of painful screams the Mage collapsed on the ground and quickly went dead, after that ordeal was finished Gabriel along with his wife and King Valarian raced over to the Prince. All was silent at the moment till finally Cedric let out a quiet groan and slowly opened his eyes; "Mother is that you?" Cedric asked weakly, the Queen and a few others who rushed to his aid looked at Cedric with shock and smiled.

"Oh my sweet child, you remember me. Thank goodness" Queen Edith cried; she then looked down at his hand and saw that his finger was gone, "oh Cedric your poor hand, I am sorry that you have to endure such pain my child" Queen Edith said with tears in her eyes. "Do not despair Mother, as long as that ring is off of my hand this pain does not concern me" Cedric stated, the Queen than gave her son a loving smile and hugged him tightly.

While the Queen and Prince continued their loving hug the King and a few others in the crowd looked at each other with concern, "what's going on, is the battle over?" questioned the King. Before anyone could reply a loud rumbling sound and a loud screeching sound echoed through the air, both Prince Cedric and Prince Gabriel looked on in shock as Brogan's body began to crumble.

Finally the Mage's body turned to dust and the only things that were left of him were his cloak and ring, when the crowd saw this they all began to cheer loudly. After the Queen helped her son to his feet Cedric looked ahead of him and smiled when he saw Gabriel, "many thanks to you my friend, I am terribly sorry for my actions. I hope you, your friends and my people can find it in your hearts to forgive me" Cedric stated sadly.

Gabriel gave his friend a friendly smile and assured him that he was not offended in any way by his actions, after the apologies were said Cedric's Father and his Squire soon appeared and happily embraced the young Prince. "We are pleased to see you back to your old self sire, are we not my King?" Paige asked the King, King Valarian gave a chuckle and nodded happily.

At that moment Cedric looked throughout his surroundings and noticed that something was missing, even though his parents and Squire were there with him his wife Amelia was nowhere to be found. "Where is the Princess, is she safe?" questioned the Prince, "do not fear my son, your wife is safely inside the castle and she's expecting" Queen Edith said happily.

After hearing the news about his wife Cedric quickly raced toward the main gate and searched every corner of the castle for her, "Cedric please calm yourself, Amelia is in her bed chambers safe and sound" Paige explained. Moments later Paige led the Prince toward his wife's bedroom and slowly opened the door, "milady, there is someone here to see you" Paige whispered.

When Cedric finally entered the room Amelia studied her husbands features and saw that he was back to normal, Cedric then noticed that his wife was holding a blanket in her arms and gave his wife a concerned stare. The Princess smiled and slowly removed the blanket to reveal a beautiful baby boy, "Cedric, I would like you to meet your new son. Xavier" Amelia said happily.

"Oh sire, your son is truly beautiful" Paige said while touching Xavier's Black hair, at that moment everyone including Gabriel and his friends hurried into the room so that they could see the baby. "You are a very lucky man Cedric, now you and I both have a son" Gabriel laughed, Cedric gave Gabriel a warm smile and happily patted his friend on the back.

Later that day after all of the damage was repaired and the wounded were healed the King and Queen held a great feast into honor their heroes, "a toast to my son Cedric and Prince Gabriel, may our people forever thank them for their courage" King Valarian exclaimed. The people then toasted their glasses and started laughing and cheering with glee; the next morning Gabriel and his friends all packed up their things for their journey home and bade farewell to their new friends.

"Have a safe journey home my friend, say hello to your parents for me won't you Gabriel?" Cedric asked, Gabriel smiled and nodded his happily. After all of their good-byes were said Gabriel and his friends hurried quickly toward Gabriel's village, the young Prince could not wait to see his loved-ones and tell his people about all of the things he saw.

"I can hardly wait to see Mother and Father again, I wonder how they are. I have forgotten that I have been gone for two and half years" Gabriel said worriedly, "don't worry Gabriel, your family will be so overjoyed to see you again. I can't wait to show them our child" Donella said while rocking Avery, suddenly Gabriel heard Vincent's sister Catrina screaming in horror and raced toward her aid.

"What's wrong Catrina, were you attacked?" Gabriel asked while gasping for breath, Catrina slowly pointed toward the horizon and revealed a horrible site. Before them all was Gabriel's village almost completely destroyed, Although Donella felt sad about her home she was nowhere near as depressed as Gabriel was. The young Elf-Prince fell to his knees and cried an endless sea of tears, "I don't know who did all this, but they will pay" Gabriel growled fiercely.

CHAPTER EIGHT

The Final Battle

As Gabriel continued crying bitter tears of sadness Donella quietly walked over to him and placed her hand on his shoulder, "do not despair Gabriel, we will find whoever did this to our kingdom and bring them to justice" Donella said reassuringly. Suddenly Gabriel and his friends were startled by a faint groaning sound coming from behind them; they rushed over to the wreckage to find an injured man groaning in pain, Vincent and the others looked at each other wondering who the man was while Donella let out a horrified gasp.

"Papa, are you all right. Who did this to you?" Donella asked frantically, the man tried his best to explain but whenever he tried to speak he coughed very loudly. "Someone give him some water, quickly" Gabriel commanded, without hesitation Kagan reached into his pouch, pulled out a canteen of water and gave it to Gabriel.

"You and Donella seem to know this man very well, is he a friend of yours?" Shegra asked. Donella gave a quick nod and went back to tending to the injured man, "please do not be offended by her silence my friends, this man is Donella's Father Sellion and he's the kingdom's Blacksmith" Gabriel informed. After Donella gave her father some water she helped him get back onto his feet, "Donella. Thank the stars you are safe" Sellion said happily in a weak voice.

"Sellion can you tell us who did this to our home?" questioned Gabriel, Sellion quickly turned his head and tried to hide the look of fear on his face. "Papa please tell us, we must know who did this to you" Donella begged her father, Sellion gave a deep sigh and prepared to tell his tale.

"About four months ago the soldiers were tending to their guard duties when all of the sudden they were attacked by a pack of reptile-like creatures, all of them appeared to be bearing the crest of Lord Throntoc and they were not alone. There were other creatures with them as well but none of the guards have ever seen them before" Sellion stated.

After hearing the name Lord Throntoc Gabriel and Donella both gasped in horror, "it can't be, there is only one being other than Lord Throntoc who would bear that symbol and he is dead" Donella exclaimed. "What of my parents are they still alive?" Gabriel asked, before Sellion could answer the skies suddenly echoed with fiendish laughter.

"Do not concern yourself with the fate of your parents Gabriel, you shall be joining them soon enough" a voice hissed, Gabriel and his friends quickly turned their heads to find a very horrifying site. Standing before them was none other than Gabriel's old nemesis Mokochu, "how can this be, you can't be alive. My friends and I saw you fall" Gabriel shouted with fear.

"That is true young Prince, I *did* fall but you seem to have forgotten one important thing. My kind have survival techniques that the likes of you have never heard of, that being said I believe the time has come for me to show you my true power" Mokochu said proudly. Hearing these words caused Gabriel and his friends to whisper in confusion, "what do you mean by 'true power' Mokochu?" Donella demanded.

Mokochu smiled fiendishly at the Princess and at that moment his whole body started to shake, suddenly Mokochu's body started to change shape and as he continued changing Mokochu soon let out a shriek so horrific that it echoed throughout every corner of the Earth. "What the deuce is he doing Gabriel?" questioned Kagan, "I have a horrible feeling that this is the new power that Mokochu spoke of" Gabriel said shakily.

When the transformation was complete Mokochu let out a loud roar and revealed to the Elf-Prince and his companions his true form. Mokochu's hair remained it's original color but his skin became rough and scaly, he had long claws on the end of his fingertips, his face looked like a crocodile and he had a long, spiked tail swinging behind him.

"You should consider this an honor Gabriel, no one has ever had the privilege of seeing me in my true form. Too bad you won't be around long enough to remember it" Mokochu hissed, "do what you will Mokochu, my friends and I have you outnumbered" Gabriel stated. Mokochu laughed at the young Elf-Prince and snapped his fingers to reveal a surprising site, the area was soon surrounded by Ackbar, Blade and many other familiar faces.

"I don't think introductions are necessary seeing as how you've already met" Mokochu laughed, "how can this be possible, how did you know about these individuals Mokochu?" Gabriel demanded. "It's quite simple my friends, after I healed myself from our first encounter I used my magic to help keep an eye on you. I was very impressed by how your skills were improving with each adventure but I was even more impressed with all of your foes" Mokochu explained.

At that moment the skies echoed loudly with the sound of evil laughter till finally Mokochu called for silence, "now the time has come for us to destroy you, have your archers ready their arrows Soraz" Mokochu commanded. Soraz smiled evilly as he and his undead soldiers readied their bows to fire; suddenly a mysterious figure arrived and struck down all of the archers with one swing of his scepter.

Mokochu glared at the figure and warned him about the rest of his army, the figure smiled at Mokochu and gave a hearty chuckle. "I haven't forgotten you my friend, that is why I brought this" the figure stated while pulling out a small orb, when the figure threw the orb on the ground it created a flash of light so bright it blinded both Mokochu and all of his allies.

"Quickly, while they're distracted follow me to safety" the figure commanded, Gabriel's eyes widened in surprise when he heard the figure's voice. "Is that you Father, thank heavens you are alive and unharmed. But where is Mother?" Gabriel asked, the figure (who was actually King Thaylog in disguise) faced the Prince and told him that all would be revealed once they were in safer quarters.

Gabriel understood his fathers words and he and his friends quickly followed the King into a secret passageway that led to a huge cave, when they arrived into the cave Gabriel and Donella were happily welcomed by a dozens of villagers, guards, servants and Queen Elbenor as well. "Oh Gabriel, my sweet child. I am so happy to see you and Donella home safe and sound" the Queen cried happily while embracing her son and daughter-in-law.

Gabriel and Donella returned the Queen's happiness with a hug of their own and once Queen Elbenor released her loved ones she soon noticed Donella holding a small child in her arms, "who is this Donella" questioned the Queen while pointing at the child. Donella gave a big smile and introduced the Queen to her new Grandchild, when the Queen saw little Avery happily cooing in Donella's arms she let out a squeal and stroked the child's hair.

After Gabriel and his friends were settled in he began to tell his parents and subjects all about their travels, when Gabriel's tale was finished his parents smiled at him happily and told him how proud they were for making so many people happy. "I appreciate your kind words Mother but we should hold our cheers until Mokochu and his allies are dead" Gabriel stated, suddenly everyone heard the sounds of loud footsteps and growling coming from outside the cave.

Everyone wondered what was making the sound but Gabriel knew all to well what it was, it was the sound of Mokochu's minions searching for them. "We must keep quiet everyone, if we stay silent they might pass us" Gabriel explained, everyone in the cave sat quietly as they nervously waited for the demons to leave and when the footsteps finally stopped all was quiet.

"I think they finally gave up" a servant whispered, everyone gave a long and silent sigh of relief believing that Mokochu had given up his search when suddenly a bright flash of green energy blasted through the entrance of the cave. When the smoke cleared the faces of evil Sorcerers Soraz and Brogan soon came into view, the two Sorcerers smiled evilly as Gabriel and his friends trembled in fear at the sight of them.

"Look how these weaklings tremble before us Brogan, it will please me greatly to have rid myself of these annoying pests" Soraz chuckled, Soraz then razed his scepter high in the air and prepared to strike when suddenly a bright light began to glow from Gabriel's chest. Everyone wondered what the light was and where it was coming from until Gabriel revealed the source of the light, he reached into his vest and pulled out the amulet that he received from the Sprites in Sunniva.

"That is a strange item you have with you Prince Gabriel, but no matter. I shall defeat you no matter what skills or objects you possess" Soraz laughed as he readied his scepter once more, just then one of the servants spotted a strange sight in the distance. Soraz and Brogan turned their heads and saw the reason for the servant's shock, in the distance was a flock of Eagles flying over their heads.

When one of the Eagles saw Gabriel being attacked it commanded the others to fly down to their aid; the King and Queen wondered why the Eagles were flying in their direction but when Gabriel saw the Eagles nearing closer he saw that their leader looked very familiar. "Fly with haste my legions, do not let those heathens harm the Prince" the leader commanded, the other Eagles obeyed their leaders commands and flew top-speed toward the cave.

As the Eagles flew closer to the cave Soraz commanded his warriors to ready their weapons, unfortunately the Eagles were flying so fast they didn't have much time to draw out their swords. Ten Eagles snatched up some of Soraz's soldiers while the rest fought with Brogan. Gabriel was relieved when he saw his old friend Scar leading them; "it is wonderful to see you Scar but I am confused, how did you know where to find me?" questioned Gabriel.

"You called for my assistance did you not?" Scar asked, Gabriel gave his friend a confused stare but quickly realized what he meant. "The amulet that was given to me by the Sprites, Princess Kendra said that it can give me the power to contact others with my mind" Gabriel stated while holding the amulet.

After he explained the powers of the amulet to his family and subjects Gabriel clasped the Amulet in his hands, closed his eyes and held it tightly to his chest. *"I call upon the amulet of Foster to ask for assistance, if any good creature can hear my words please come to my kingdom's aid. We beseech you"* Gabriel thought, Gabriel's thoughts were interrupted when he heard screeching sounds coming from behind.

Gabriel turned around to find one of Scar's Eagles being attacked by Ackbar and Mokochu, "calm down now little birdie, someone could get hurt" Ackbar laughed while pulling on Scar's wings. Gabriel glared at Ackbar and prepared to draw his sword when suddenly his father stepped in and stopped everyone from fighting any further, "halt, cease this violence at once. If we must fight one another Mokochu I suggest we do like honorable warriors" King Thaylog stated.

Everyone stared at the King in confusion and wondered what he was planning, but Mokochu knew all too well what the King meant and reluctantly agreed to his terms. "As you wish Thaylog, we will meet in the empty valley outside the kingdom's walls at sunrise. Until then, farewell" Mokochu growled angrily, when Mokochu and his warriors left everyone looked at the King and wondered what he had planned to stop them.

"But sire, how are we going to stop Mokochu. He has already decimated many of our bravest soldiers" a guard cried, King Thaylog turned his gaze toward the guard and lowered his head in sadness. "I...don't know, I fear that our forces have become too weak to stop him. However that doesn't mean that I'm going to give up without a fight, no matter what happens tomorrow Mokochu *will* fall" the King shouted, everyone raised their hands high in the air and started to cheer loudly.

Upon seeing this Gabriel raced over to his father and hugged him tightly, "I knew you wouldn't give up that easily father, with you leading us I know we can win the battle" Gabriel said with a smile. Later that night everyone who was able to fight gathered at the Blacksmith shop to receive their weaponry and armor while Gabriel and his friends prepared themselves in the castle's Weapons Hall, after all of their legions were prepared they returned to their sleeping chambers for a goodnights rest.

The next morning King Thaylog and his forces arrived at the outskirts of the kingdom and prepared for Mokochu's arrival, as the sun continued to rise a strange sound started to echo through the skies. It was the sound of Mokochu's Reptiliac warriors marching and growling in the distance, the sound was so horrid it made many of the King's warriors quiver in fright. "Stand firm everyone, no matter what we must not let Mokochu win" the King stated, as Mokochu's army neared closer to them everyone tried their best to remain brave but the thought of the imminent battle still frightened them.

"Leave none alive, I have no interest in capturing prisoners" Mokochu commanded, at that moment Mokochu's creatures let out a loud roar and charged toward the Kings army. "Forward men, for the glory of Overon" the King shouted, the King then unsheathed his sword and commanded his army to charge. When the King's command was heard all of the warriors of Overon drew out their weapons and charged toward Mokochu's forces, the battle cries of both armies echoed fiercely through the morning sky till finally both sides collided.

The battle waged on for what seemed like an eternity and it appeared that the Kings army had the upper hand, "keep fighting everyone, leave none of them standing" Gabriel screamed as he swung his blade at multiple Reptiliac warriors. Suddenly Blade appeared from behind Gabriel and tackled hum to the ground, the young Prince tried to break free but Blade's grip on him was too strong. "Go on and squeal, little one. Your friends can't help you this time" Blade chuckled.

As Blade prepared his weapon for the final blow Gabriel closed his eyes and prepared for the worse, at that moment the sounds of war-horns echoed throughout the skies and the people started to wonder if it was more of Mokochu's warriors coming to his aid. Gabriel's heart lifted when he saw his friend Cedric standing among the ranks, standing alongside with Cedric were his parents, his wife Amelia, Porthos, Miria, Clortho, the Great Dragon and many of their other friends and allies.

"Prince Gabriel requires our aid, we must go to him at once" Prince Cedric shouted, with that command said all of the armies charged toward the battle with great speed. Soon the hilltop was swarming with creatures of all different sorts, there were Humans, Dragons, Sprites, Fairies, Pixies, Nymphs, Centaurs and so much more.

Gabriel thanked God that the amulet delivered his message to them and now his strength and courage returned to him tenfold, when the armies arrived at that the battlefield the tide quickly turned for the worse for Mokochu and his legions. Soon Mokochu's allies reduced to nothing and many of his warriors have either fallen or retreated, "NO, I CANNOT LOSE. VICTORY WAS ALMOST MINE!" Mokochu shrieked. Upon hearing Mokochu's pitiful cries of defeat Gabriel took his attention off the remaining Reptiliac warriors and turned his attention to him, "no please, have mercy. Please spare me young Prince" Mokochu cried.

Gabriel glared at Mokochu and began to march toward him, "you dare ask me for mercy, after you put the woman I love in danger, nearly reduced my kingdom to ruin and tried to harm my family you have the *audacity* to ask me for mercy...never" Gabriel growled. He then lifted his sword high into the air and plunged it deep into Mokochu's chest, when he pulled his sword out Gabriel then sliced off Mokochu's head making sure that there would be no chance of him healing himself ever again.

When they all saw their young Prince strike down Mokochu the people of Overon along with all of their allies cheered loudly for his victory, at that moment something miraculous happened. After Mokochu was dead the whole kingdom immediately returned to it's natural beauty and all of the destruction that Mokochu caused vanished, later that day after everyone's wounds were healed and the land was cleansed of the stench of death everyone gathered inside the palace for an important announcement.

The King and Queen led everyone into a large hall filled with large statues of many ancient warriors, when everyone reached the middle of the hall there were over a dozen new statues standing alongside the others. Everyone loved the new additions to the Hall of Legends but were even more overjoyed when they saw a statue of Prince Gabriel as well, after everyone showed their appreciation for the kingdoms heroes King Thaylog stood before them all and began to speak.

"This is a great day for Overon and all of our allies, now that Mokochu and his warriors are vanquished our kingdom can once again be at peace. On that note let these statues be a gift of thanks to our Prince and his friends, in honor of their great victory. Now they will be placed in this hall alongside the greatest heroes in all of Overon, may their legacy live long in the hearts of future generations" The King said happily.

After King Thaylog finished his speech all of the townspeople cheered loudly for Gabriel and his friends while King and Queen embraced their son in a loving hug, when his parents finally released him Gabriel smiled happily and faced his wife. "Now that Mokochu is dead and all of his evil influence is gone our people can live peacefully once more" Gabriel said with a smile, later that night King Thaylog and Queen Elbenor held a great feast in honor of their victory.

"A toast to our brave warriors, may the peace they've brought us last until the stars rain down from the skies" the King exclaimed, after the toast was made everyone quickly ate their fill and danced merrily around the dining hall. While their friends and family danced in the hall Gabriel and Donella sat outside on the balcony looking at the stars, as the merriment continued behind them Gabriel faced his wife and placed a small flower in her hair.

Donella looked at the flower in her hair and smiled happily, "now our lives can truly begin my love, now our *peoples* lives can truly begin" Gabriel said while looking down at the village. Gabriel then turned to his wife and kissed her passionately, after he released Donella from his embrace he smiled at her knowing that from that day on peace would remain in Overon and its neighbors till the end of their days.

The End

Printed in the United States
77445LV00004B/487-504

9 781425 981204